SHERIFF OF JACK HOLLOW

SHERIFF OF JACK HOLLOW

Lee Hoffman

SAGEBRUSH
Large Print Westerns

First published in Great Britain by Hale
First published in the United States by Dell Books

Published in Large Print 2006 by ISIS Publishing Ltd.,
7 Centremead, Osney Mead, Oxford OX2 0ES
United Kingdom
by arrangement with
Golden West Literary Agency

British Library Cataloguing in Publication Data
Hoffman, Lee, 1932–
    Sheriff of Jack Hollow. –
    Large print ed. –
    (Sagebrush Western series)
    1. Western stories
    2. Large type books
    I. Title
    813.5'4 [F]

ISBN–10 0–7531–7553–3 (hb)
ISBN–13 978–0–7531–7553–8 (hb)

Printed and bound in Great Britain by
T. J. International Ltd., Padstow, Cornwall

To Alan Grofield, anyway

CHAPTER ONE

Abe Ludlow was sweeping up when Tuck Tobin walked into his barber shop. He grinned at Tuck. "Morning, Sheriff."

"Morning, Abe," Tuck said. He settled into the chair and leaned back. "Shave."

"Trim?" Abe asked as he wrapped the cloth around Tuck's neck.

Tuck shook his head.

Looking doubtful, Abe said, "Your moustache is getting kinda scraggly. You know, Tuck, when a man's up for reelection, it doesn't hurt any to keep up appearances."

Tuck grunted. He supposed Abe was right. It seemed like damned foolishness that a man's looks would count against him in an election. It should be what he did that counted.

"Curly Hobbs was in this morning," Abe said. "You just missed him by a couple of minutes."

Tuck grunted again.

Abe continued, "You know, Tuck, I got a notion Curly's out for your job."

Tuck had the same notion. Just yesterday he'd run into Curly, and Curly'd got to ragging him about his

1

age, like turning forty was the end of a man. Curly was just twenty-five, and had a notion that was a man's prime. Tuck allowed a man might be quicker at twenty-five, but at forty he had more horse sense. Tuck figured these days horse sense and experience counted for more than a fast gun.

Ten years ago, it had been different. Back then, Tuck was deputy town marshal and Jack Hollow was one hell of a town. Now Tuck was sheriff of Isaac County, and Jack Hollow was so tame it didn't need a deputy to the town marshal. Curly Hobbs handled the marshal's job with a glad hand and a hearty grin. Tuck felt due credit for that. He'd helped tame the town. He rode herd on the county. Curly was riding his coattails. And now Curly was talking him down, like he was too old and worn out to do his job.

To hell with Curly Hobbs, he thought. But he told Abe to go ahead and trim his hair and moustache.

Abe finished scraping Tuck's jaw. He had his scissors out and was snipping at Tuck's neat red moustache when the shouting began.

Gesturing Abe's hand away, Tuck started out of the chair. "What the hell is that?"

Abe darted to the door and squinted out. He answered, "Something going on down the street. I can't see what, but it's sure drawing a crowd."

Tuck flung the barber cloth on the chair and pushed past Abe to stride out the door. Abe hurried after him.

The crowd was three blocks down. As Tuck and Abe passed the Great Western Commercial and Cattlemen's Bank, Charlie Willis, the bank manager, came trotting

2

out. Joining them, he asked, "What's going on down there?"

Tuck shrugged.

"It sounds like a couple of she-cats faced up on a back fence," Abe said.

Charlie grinned and suggested, "Or a couple of whores from Ida Red's having a difference of opinion."

"Same thing." Abe chuckled.

They followed in Tuck's wake as he shoved through to the front of the crowd. In the midst of the cheering spectators they found Eustacia Kogh and Rowena Greenwood going at each other like a pair of she-cats, all teeth and claws and yowling.

Stacy Kogh, part Cherokee, was tall and dark, and usually stately and immaculate. Now she was disheveled, savage, crouching like a cougar ready to spring.

Her burgundy morning suit was in dusty disarray. Her bonnet with its frills of white egret plumes was underfoot, the feathers trampled. Her glistening black coif leaned precariously, spilling hairpins. She spat epithets at Weenie.

Weenie Greenwood was the china doll of Ida Red's collection. She was small and blonde, a delicate, helpless-looking creature in lace and frills. Now she looked like an angry child, her lips in a pout, her little hands in fists. Her straw bonnet with its pink posies hung from the side of her head by its hatpin. The frills on her shirtwaist heaved with her gasping.

"Oh hell," Tuck muttered. He scanned the crowd. Curly Hobbs was in the forefront. Working up to

Curly's side, Tuck said, "Hadn't you better break it up, Marshal?"

Curly grinned, flashing white teeth. His blue eyes twinkled. He ran his fingers through thick black hair. "Why?" he said. "Let'em have their fun."

"That's a *street brawl* they're having," Tuck answered.

"I mean the crowd." Curly gave a nod toward the spectators. "The girls aren't hurting each other, and folks are enjoying the show."

Behind Tuck, Charlie Willis agreed. "There's no harm in it."

Abe Ludlow said, "It ain't like they don't do it all the time over at the cathouse."

Tuck turned away from them. He looked at the women.

Snarling, Stacy launched herself at Weenie. Her long nails were aimed at Weenie's throat. Weenie jerked back, and Stacy's claws caught frills. They ripped open the whole front of Weenie's shirtwaist.

The crowd cheered.

A bunch of cowboys, watching from horseback, raised a wild yapping of approval.

Charlie Willis nudged Tuck in the ribs and chuckled.

Tuck wondered if he was the only one in the whole bunch who didn't find it all very funny.

Weenie caught the front of Stacy's jacket and jerked so hard that its buttons flew off. Stacy swung a hand in an open slap. It smacked against Weenie's cheek. Weenie swung back. She connected. Stacy squealed. Stacy struck again, and Weenie shrieked. Her hatpin gave up, and her bonnet tumbled off. Lunging, Stacy gripped both hands deep into Weenie's honey curls.

"Tail 'er, Stacy!" one of the cowboys whooped. "Tail 'er down!"

Stacy wrenched at the curls and flung a hip deftly against Weenie's side.

Weenie went down.

Somebody fired off a gun.

Dammit, even if the girls didn't hurt each other, Tuck thought, those fool cowboys always hoorawing with firearms might. He told Curly, "You want this mob getting out of hand? If you don't break it up, something's sure as hell gonna happen. Somebody will get hurt."

"You're getting spooky in your old age, Tuck," Curly answered. He chuckled. Charlie and Abe joined him.

Tuck felt a warmth in his face. He wanted to tell them forty wasn't so damned old. Hell, Charlie was at least forty, and Abe was pushing it. But he damned sure wasn't going to let Curly get a rise out of him. Mouth taut, he looked at the women.

Weenie was on her back, and Stacy was astraddle her. Stacy's fingers were clutched in the tangles of Weenie's hair. Rocking back and forth with Weenie's head between her hands, Stacy looked like she was using Weenie's skull to pound nails into the boardwalk.

Suddenly Weenie whimpered, "You're *hurting* me!"

"Dammit!" Tuck said. "Somebody's got to stop this!"

"No," Charlie Willis protested as Tuck started toward the women.

"Help!" someone hollered. "Help! The bank's been robbed!"

Pete Keeley was standing on the top step of the Great Western Commercial and Cattlemen's Bank. He waved the pistol he'd just fired for attention, and screamed for help.

The crowd that had been watching Stacy and Weenie milled a moment in confusion. Then it broke and raced toward the bank.

In a couple of strides, Tuck Tobin had taken the lead. He bounded up the bank's steps two at a time. As he reached the top step, he noted smugly that Curly Hobbs, just behind him, was breathing heavily from the quick sprint. Young or not, Curly was soft.

"The bank's been robbed!" Pete Keeley repeated to the two of them.

People were pushing up the steps for a look. Tuck glowered at them. "Keep back! Charlie? Where's Charlie Willis?"

"Here!" the bank manager answered as he hurried up the steps. His face was pale, sheened with sudden perspiration. "Tuck, you've got to —"

"Hold on a minute," Tuck interrupted. He looked at Curly. "It happened in town. It's in Curly's jurisdiction."

Curly nodded. But he said, "Likely they're out of town and in the county by now. That makes it *your* jurisdiction."

"You want me to handle it?" Tuck asked.

"If you feel up to it."

Curly just didn't want any part of it, Tuck thought. Curly was a politician, not a lawman. He wondered if folks would ever learn to tell the difference. Accepting the responsibility, he looked out at the crowd. He spotted Glenn Hotchkiss, the blacksmith. He'd used Glenn as a temporary deputy in the past. He called, "Glenn, keep this mob in order. Don't let anybody get into the bank."

"Right!" Glenn shouted back.

Tuck turned to Pete Keeley. "What happened?"

"I don't know. I just came to take care of some business —" Keeley looked hopefully at Charlie Willis. "It's about my mortgage. I *got* to have an extension."

"Damn your mortgage! What about the robbery?" Charlie snapped.

Keeley scowled at him. "I don't know nothing about the robbery."

"Pete, what happened?" Tuck said.

Keeley turned and spoke to him. "I went inside and seen Shorty in there, all trussed up like a calf for cutting. The safe's open. There's coin scattered around the floor."

Wheeling, Tuck strode into the bank.

The teller, Shorty Carlisle, was lying on the floor, his hands and feet lashed tight with piggin string. A bandana had been stuffed into his mouth, and another tied over it. He made chest-deep grunting sounds as Tuck hurried toward him. Dropping to one knee, Tuck pulled away the gag.

"Shorty, what happened?" Tuck asked.

Shorty coughed and sputtered. He gasped, "Untie me!"

Tuck hunted out his clasp knife, bit it open, and sawed at the cords on Shorty's wrists. As he cut, he asked again, "What happened?"

"Three of them," Shorty said, still gasping. "Whooping big bastards in dusters. Guns. Made me open the safe. Cleaned it out. Oh, hell!"

"Did you get a look at them?"

"No, their faces were covered. Hats down low."

Tuck jerked loose the cords that had bound Shorty's hands and set to work on his ankles. Charlie Willis and Curly Hobbs were standing behind Tuck, watching. Shorty looked up at Charlie. Rubbing his wrists, he repeated, "Oh, hell!"

Charlie nodded slowly, wordlessly. His face was grim white. He bent to pick up a quarter dollar that lay near his feet. He set it on the desk. He turned to Tuck. "Do something."

Tuck nodded. He made a final slash at Shorty's bonds, pulled them away, and rose. Returning to the door, he looked out.

The crowd was bunched up, waiting for something more to happen. A half dozen cowboys watched from horseback. Tuck looked at the cowboys. "You Texicans know how to track?"

An old-timer with a face as wrinkled as a raisin worked up spit, let fly, and allowed, "I reckon I can tell which way a cow's went."

"Track men?" Tuck asked.

The old-timer nodded.

8

The younger cowhands exchanged glances and grins and agreed among themselves that they could do as much.

"Want to ride for the law?" Tuck asked them.

Charlie Willis had come to his side. Charlie called, "There's ten dollars a man in it for you! And five hundred to the man who brings the bastards back!"

The cowboys whooped their willingness.

"Then suppose — let's see — you two ride the road out east," Tuck said. He made a chopping motion of his hand, separating two cowpokes from the bunch. He chopped off the next two. "You ride the road out to the west. See if you can pick up tracks on the road, or maybe turning off it somewheres. Likely three horses, traveling real fast."

Two cowboys remained. Tuck told them, "You fellers ride circle around the town, see if you can raise their sign off the road."

Shouting, the cowboys started to spur their mounts.

"Hold on a minute, dammit!" Tuck hollered at them.

They drew rein and looked back at him.

"All of you, raise your right hands." He lifted his own in demonstration. They imitated him. He figured there wasn't time or need for fancy formalities. He said simply, "All right, you're all official deputies now. You're under orders from me. You find sign, you send word back here. I'll have a posse ready to take to the trail. Now go."

The cowboys whooped and lit out.

Tuck turned to Glenn Hotchkiss. "Glenn, you hold up your right hand. All right, you're deputized. Round up a dozen good men and get them all armed and mounted. Vittled, too. We might have a piece of riding ahead of us. We'll meet in front of the courthouse."

"Yes, sir!" Glenn agreed.

A soft murmur sounded from the crowd. Men began to melt away from its edges.

There were always plenty of people on hand to watch trouble happen, Tuck thought as he turned his back on them. Not nearly so many handy when it came to doing something about trouble.

"What are *you* going to do?" Curly Hobbs asked him. "Take it easy while those cowboys bring them in?"

"I'm going to outfit myself," Tuck said coldly. "I'm going to see to it there's a decent posse shaped up. And I'm going to hope those cowboys turn up sign for us to follow real quick."

As Tuck strode off toward the county stable, Curly called after him, "Good luck, old pal."

The three men who galloped hurriedly out of Jack Hollow headed west on the wagon road as far as Hockett Creek. There they turned off. Splashing into the water, they headed north.

The creek lay in a deep gully with stands of cotton-wood and chokecherry lining its banks. It was shadowy in the gully, and they were well hidden from sight.

Collin McKay was the last man in line. Bull Bordeaux was up front, with the saddlebags full of money bouncing behind his cantle. Lyle Bordeaux,

Bull's kid brother, was close behind him. All three were riding bay horses and wearing linen dusters.

The horse Collin rode was a long-legged gelding he'd picked because it had speed and endurance and its common color wouldn't attract attention. But it was young and skittish, and it had been acting up the whole time. Now, with water splashing around its hooves and Collin's duster flapping at the edge of its vision, it was downright jumpy. At every stride, water splashed and linen flapped and the horse gave a shy.

Now that the robbing was done and there was no telling who'd be on their trail, or when, Collin was feeling jumpy himself. The continual shying was getting on his nerves. At last he hollered at the Bordeaux brothers, "Hey, wait a minute!"

Both drew rein and looked back at him. Bull called, "What's the matter?"

"This damned horse," Collin said. "Every time my damned coat flaps the damned horse wants to hightail it."

"Peel the duster," Bull said.

"That's what I'm doing," Collin answered. He'd started to shrug out of it, but that was upsetting the horse even worse. He worked the reins as it danced under him, and realized he'd have to dismount to get out of the duster, or the horse would likely go into wall-eyed fits.

Stepping down while the Bordeaux boys watched was somehow embarrassing. Afoot, Collin turned his back to them and pulled the duster off.

Bull chuckled just the way Collin had expected, like it was a sign of weakness or something for him to have to dismount.

Collin was out of the duster and cramming it into his saddlebag when it occurred to Lyle to take off his own duster. He'd shucked one arm out of a sleeve when his horse gave a lurch that almost unseated him. With a curse, he climbed down to finish the job.

Collin chuckled then. Remounting, he reined over to Bull's side and asked, "How much you reckon we got?"

"Lot of paper money," Bull said. He gave the stuffed saddlebag an affectionate caress. "Big bills."

"Paper's good these days," Collin said. "How much you reckon it adds up to?"

"Maybe thirty thousand," Bull speculated.

Collin whistled through his teeth. He touched his fingertips as he calculated then said, "That's around six thousand for each of us. That's a hell of a lot of money."

Lyle had his duster stowed and was in the saddle again. Stepping his horse to his brother's side, he said, "I've been thinking about that."

"About what?" Bull asked him.

"I mean, after all, what did those girls do to earn equal shares with the rest of us?"

"They came up with the whole plan in the first place," Collin answered. "They dreamed up the job and they called us in to do it and they distracted everybody in town while we took the money and got out with our hides whole. That's what they did."

"They didn't take the chance we took," Lyle protested. "They didn't stand to get their tails shot off like we did. We did the work, and now we're on the run and they're back cozy in the whorehouse."

"Brother Lyle's got something there," Bull said.

Lyle nodded. "It ain't like we couldn't have done the job without them. But they sure as hell couldn't have done it without us."

"It was *their* plan," Collin insisted. "We couldn't even of thought of it without them."

"We've robbed banks before," Bull said. "Didn't need no women to plan for us."

"Parker planned for us then," Collin said. "You reckon you're smart enough to rob a bank without somebody planned it for you?"

The scowl Bull gave him made Collin sorry he'd said that. Bull was an ugly man, with ugly ways. Collin knew others he'd a damn sight sooner have worked with. But Bull and Lyle had been the only ones he'd been able to get hold of for this job. And they were real good at bank robbing.

"You got to admit the girls did their part," he said.

Lyle put in, "Minnie would have helped us and never asked for a share."

"Minnie, Minnie, Minnie!" Collin snapped. "I'm sick and tired of hearing about that whore of yours."

"Minnie's no whore!" Lyle sounded indignant at the idea.

"Like hell. She's in a whorehouse right now, ain't she?"

"Madam Bailey's just taking care of her for me while I'm away from Morrison on business," Lyle answered.

"If I know old Bailey," Collin said, "she's got your precious Minnie working her tail off while you're away —"

"Every penny Minnie earns, Bailey's holding for me!"

"— and if I know your precious Minnie, she's loving every minute of it."

"You shut up about Minnie!" Lyle shouted.

"Both of you shut up about Minnie," Bull said. "She ain't no part of this. We were talking about how we're gonna slice up this bank money."

"Five ways, like we agreed from the start," Collin said.

"Why?" Bull asked, his tone mocking. "What are those little gals gonna do if we don't pony up shares for them? They can't run to the law without they singe their own tailfeathers. You reckon they're gonna load up their garter guns and come hunting us down?"

Lyle chuckled at the picture. "You afraid of those whores, Coll?"

"They got a fair share coming."

"We got a fair share coming," Bull answered.

Lyle said, "Poor Coll, running and hiding up the owlhoot trail with them fierce women after him."

Collin didn't want to argue. He didn't want to get mad. Tautly, he said, "Weenie Greenwood is my friend. I don't mean to double-deal her."

14

"I say we split it three ways, not five," Bull grumbled. "If you want, Coll, you can share yours with the whores."

Lyle nodded vigorously in agreement.

"Dammit!" Collin found himself shouting. "You never tried nothing like this the other jobs we did together."

"Other jobs we did together we were all working for Parker," Bull answered. "And *he* wouldn't have put up with nothing like this."

"You figure *I'll* put up with it, huh?" Collin said through his teeth.

Bull nodded knowingly. "Coll, you're a good man at what you do, but you ain't nowhere the man Parker is. You ain't the man Lyle or me is. You'll back down if it comes to a showdown, and you know it. You'll take what me and Lyle says. And we say the hell with the women."

Collin swallowed hard. He had a sick sort of feeling that Bull might be right. He hesitated, his lips making a move but finding no words to answer with.

"Well now," Bull said with a trace of a smile. "Let's us just —"

"Hey, brother! Coll!" Lyle interrupted. He was holding his head high, tilted slightly to one side. His eyes were wide. "You hear something?"

"What?" Bull asked.

"Horses."

Collin cocked an ear. He caught the sound. He grunted, "Damn!"

Bull told Lyle, "Take a look, see if you can spot 'em."

Turning his horse, Lyle rode slowly up the sloped bank of the gulley. He neared the top and reined in. Rising in the stirrups, he peered over the brink. He poised a moment, stock-still. Then, with a bob of his head, he wheeled and hurried down again.

"Riders on a ridge!"

"How many?"

"I only seen a couple of 'em. Could be more, though. Could be scouting for a posse."

Bull nodded as he slapped spurs to his mount. "Let's move!"

Bull was in the lead as they raced up the creek. Suddenly he gave a jerk of the reins, swinging his mount into a dry wash that opened into one side of the gully. Lyle raced after him.

Collin's bay was on the off lead, and the wash was on the nigh side. As Collin laid his rein along the bay's neck, the horse tried to switch leads. Legs crossing, it stumbled.

Collin felt it falling. Kicking free of the stirrups, he jumped. He hit the ground shoulder first, rolling. He came to a stop face down in the creek.

As he rose to his knees he saw his horse struggling to get up. For an instant, he thought it was going to succeed. Then he saw jagged bone poking through the hide of one foreleg. Blood spurted, spreading pale pink stains in the water.

"Oh damn," he mumbled to himself. He looked toward the Bordeaux brothers and shouted, "Hold up! Hey, hold up there!"

16

They both stopped and looked back. Bull lifted rein, walking his mount toward Collin.

Collin pulled the Army Remington from his holster. Leveling it at the bay's head, he drew back the hammer and let it slip.

As lead slammed into its skull, the horse made a strangling sound. Its struggle stopped. Its head fell heavily to the ground. It lay still, partly in the dry wash, partly in the creek.

Gesturing at Bull with the hand that held the gun, Collin scrambled to his feet. He started to run toward Bull. He intended to vault up onto the horse behind Bull. He knew it might slow them some riding double. But —

He saw the drawn gun in Bull's hand. It was pointed at him.

"Damn fool," Bull said quietly.

At the sight of the aimed gun, Collin dove for cover. He dropped to roll and hide himself behind the dead horse.

Bull's gun blasted as Collin moved. Collin felt a kick against his side. Gasping, he sprawled behind the carcass. His own gun was in his hand. He snapped a shot in Bull's direction. Even as he fired, he knew it was wild.

Bull fired again. Lead slapped into the body of the horse.

"Bull!" Lyle called. "Bull, the riders! They'll hear!"

With a nod to himself, Bull threw one more hurried shot at Collin, wheeled his mount, and flung it into a run up the dry wash.

Collin rose to his knees. His side felt numb. His hand shook as he thumbed back the hammer and tried to take aim at Bull's broad back.

He'd never killed a man before.

He hesitated.

And then Bull had disappeared around a bend of the dry wash.

Collin eased down the Remington's hammer. Sighing, he hauled himself to his feet. He dropped the gun into its holster, then touched his fingertips to his left side. They found blood. But there was no pain. And his arms and legs all worked. He didn't think he was hurt bad. He could stop the bleeding with his bandana. Take care of the wound himself. He'd be all right.

First, he had to get the hell away before somebody showed up to find out what all the shooting was about.

CHAPTER
TWO

By chance, Pike found himself paired up with the Kid, riding west out of Jack Hollow in search of sign.

The Kid was eager, on his first trip uptrail from brasada country. He rode in the lead, hanging out of his saddle, staring at the ground.

Pike rode easy, slumping with his chin on his chest. He held the reins loosely in a knobby hand that rested against a gaunt thigh. Pike had been the runt of his maw's litter, a wiry tough youngun who had grown into a wiry tough man. As a hunter, a trader, a mustanger, and a rough string rider, he figured he'd broken every bone in his body at least twice, some three or four times. He'd lost most of his teeth in brawls. He claimed it was jealous women who'd thinned his hair. Now he was as gnarled as a bristlecone pine. And still as wiry tough as ever.

He looked like he might be dozing in the saddle. He didn't lift his head. Occasionally he blinked and scanned the scenery. Unlike the Kid, he didn't bother looking for the marks of horseshoes. He hunted mounds of horse droppings. He knew a good healthy horse dropped eight, maybe ten times a day. Robbers would be riding good, healthy, well-fed, well-rested horses. Three horses like that all getting worked out in the morning ought to have left plenty of sign.

It wasn't sign Pike spotted. It was riders. Four of them coming out of a distant draw.

The Kid saw them and shouted, "Hey! Hey, look yonder! It's them! It's the robbers!"

Pike worked his jaw, spat, and answered, "Like hell."

"Huh?"

"That's Chuck and Dude from our outfit, and a couple of strange hairpins."

The Kid squinted at the riders. He could see their shapes but not their faces. He said, "You're only guessing."

"I am, am I?" Pike grumbled, mildly amused. "Wait and see."

He had no mind to share his secrets with a sassy green pup like the Kid. Truth was, the years were making him farsighted. He figured it was a blessing. A man like Pike needed to see what was at a distance a lot more than he needed to see the end of his own nose.

He could make out distinctly that one rider was on a patchy pinto. A clever robber would never ride an eye-catching horse like that. But Chuck had been on a patchy pinto when the sheriff sent him and Dude to circle the town. Dude was on a light sorrel, and one of the distant figures had a light sorrel under him. That made it Chuck and Dude, and Pike figured two asscolts like Chuck and Dude weren't likely to catch a pair of desperate outlaws without a shot being fired. There'd been no sound of gunfire. So the other two were likely just strangers Chuck and Dude had run into along the way.

The Kid felt his face redden as he saw that two of them were, indeed, Chuck and Dude. Slamming his horse into a gallop, racing to meet them, he shouted, "Likely the other two are the robbers!"

Pike lifted rein and followed after him at a lope.

Chuck and Dude were riding tense, their faces grim. They carried drawn revolvers. The strangers with them wore empty holsters.

"What you got there?" the Kid called. He looked at the bared guns and grinned broadly. "You caught them!"

"Might be," Chuck said.

Dude gave a nod.

"No!" one of the strangers protested. "We ain't robbers!"

The other nodded agreement.

They halted together, with Chuck on one side of the strangers and Dude on the other. The Kid faced them. Coming up beside the Kid, Pike surveyed the captives.

Both were fresh shaven, well scrubbed, and slicked up with clean shirts and new bandanas. From their rigs and their mounts, Pike knew they were out of Texas. The one who'd spoken had a natural-born Texas drawl.

"I'm Pete Jones," the stranger was saying. He aimed a thumb at his companion. "This here is Waco Bowman. He don't talk much. We're from down Texas, come up with a herd. It's holding now over northwest aways behind Hockett's Creek."

Pike nodded. He knew there was a herd up that way. He figured the two were exactly what they claimed to be and nothing more. Glancing from Chuck to Dude, he said, "You really reckon they're the robbers?"

"Don't know," Chuck allowed. "Me and Dude were riding around the way the sheriff told us when we came on them. We reckoned we'd better take them in and make sure."

At the same time, Pete Jones was saying, "We're nighthawks, only just got off work. We were heading into town to cut loose our wolves. We don't know nothing about any bank robbery."

Pike aimed his gaze at Chuck's gun. "Give you a fight, did they?"

Chuck answered with an embarrassed shake of his head.

Eagerly, the Kid said, "There's supposed to be three of 'em. Where's the other one?"

"Off with the other two, I'd say," Pike grunted.

Pete Jones suggested, "While you're messing around with us, the ones you want are getting away."

"Uh huh," Pike agreed.

In the distance, something exploded.

"That was a gunshot!" the Kid shouted.

"*There*," Pete said, as if the sound confirmed his claim. "There, you see? There's your robbers."

"Handgun," Pike commented. "Newfangled cartridge revolver. Colt's or Remington's, most likely."

Dude looked uncertainly at the prisoners. He suggested, "Maybe it's just somebody hunting."

22

"It was back the way you two come from," Chuck said to Pete Jones. "You see anybody hunting back that way?"

"Never noticed nobody," Pete Jones answered.

Two more shots sounded, one right after the other. Then another.

"Come on!" the Kid shouted, wheeling to gallop off and see. Chuck and Dude hurried after him, with Dude insisting it must be a hunter.

Another shot.

"It's the robbers, all right," Pete Jones said as he and Waco Bowman spurred their mounts to follow.

Nodding to himself, Pike lifted rein and went along.

They reached the gully and skidded their mounts down the bank into Hockett's Creek. Pointing upstream, Chuck shouted, "Look there!"

Lying in the creek, its head up a dry wash, its body in the water, was a bay horse. It looked dead. The saddle was still on its back. An open saddlebag was spilling linen.

Chuck swung down off his mount. He tugged at the cloth and held up a linen duster.

"Robbers!" Pete said very definitely. This time no one disagreed with him.

Dude eyed the horse and said, "It busted a leg."

"That explains the shooting," the Kid said.

Pike only grunted to himself. He thought any fool should know it didn't take five shots to put an end to an injured horse. And a man who walked away from a downed mount didn't generally leave his saddle soaking in a creek unless he was in one hell of a hurry.

It was Pete Jones's silent partner, Waco Bowman, who drifted slowly around the carcass, studying the ground. He stopped at the mouth of the dry wash, dismounted, and looked closely at the mud. Curious, the others all bunched around him. All except Pike. Still aboard his horse, Pike sat off aways, letting them play their games.

"Two horses," Waco announced sullenly, as if he resented spending the words. "Went up this way at a run."

"That's them!" the Kid hollered. "Let's get 'em! Come on!" He flung himself onto his mount and lit out up the wash.

The others hurried after him. All but Pike.

Once they were on their way, and out of his way, Pike slipped down from the saddle and squatted to examine such tracks as they hadn't ridden over and muddled completely.

Now his farsightedness was a bother to him. Even so, he could tell both horses had been ridden, one a little heavier loaded than the other. But neither had enough weight on it to be carrying two men.

He returned to the carcass in the creek. It had one bullet in its head and another in its back. He reckoned the broken leg had come first, and the slug in its head had put the horse out of its misery. From the lay of the hole in its back, that bullet had been fired after it was down.

Somebody had been astraddle the dead horse before it went down. He hadn't ridden away. He wasn't still here. So he had gone off afoot.

Five shots had been fired. Two bullets had gone into the horse. Three had gone other places.

"Two hairpins shooting at each other," Pike said aloud. He opined that somewhere there was a man afoot, maybe with lead in him, and likely that man was a bank robber whose partners hadn't felt like hauling him along once he'd lost his horse.

Pike asked himself what he'd do in a spot like that. He answered himself that he'd hide his tracks the best he could and head for a hole. The best way to hide the tracks would be to plant them under the running water of the creek.

Remounting, he headed up Hockett Creek, watching its bank for sign of a man climbing out of it.

The numbness was wearing away. Collin McKay's side was beginning to ache. And he was tired. Hungry and tired and a bit giddy.

He wasn't sure how far he'd come up the creek, but he thought he could afford himself a few moments' rest. With a sigh, he slumped down onto a windfallen log and began to take stock.

Bull Bordeaux's bullet had kicked him in the left side. It had cut through the row of cartridge loops on his gun belt before it sliced into his flesh. He was thankful the loops had been empty. If he'd had rounds in them, the slug might have set them off. That could have been plenty serious.

As it was, the thicknesses of leather had taken a lot of punch out of the slug. Going in at an angle, it had peeled enough of his hide to spill blood. Then it had gone on. A small wound. He'd been shot a lot worse than that before.

Still, he'd a sight sooner the bullet had missed him altogether. His side throbbed like a toothache. The blood had trickled along his crotch and down the inside of his leg. He felt sticky with it. And he was hungry.

He had to find a place to rest and tend the wound properly. And something to put into his belly. After that, he needed a horse so he could light out after the Bordeaux brothers.

Damn them!

He'd trusted them. He'd led Weenie Greenwood and her girlfriend to trust them. He felt rotten about that. He owed it to the girls to square things. He had to find the Bordeaux boys and collect from them for himself and the girls. And more to boot.

He wondered if he really would, or if Bull Bordeaux had been right about him and when it came to a showdown he'd back water.

There was only one way to find out.

He heaved himself to his feet and started walking again.

Ahead, an old path sloped down the bank of the gully. He looked thoughtfully at it. It had to lead somewhere. A house maybe. Food and rest. Or capture.

Gun in hand, he cautiously climbed the path. He discovered that it led from the creek bank across a hardpack yard to the grassy mound of a sod house. Cottonwoods clustered around the house. Beyond them, he could make out another structure, likely a barn. An ordinary prairie farm. Except that there was

26

no one in sight, and no chickens or cattle or hogs ranged the yard. The place seemed deserted.

It wouldn't do as a hole to hide in. A posse would stop and check it out for sure. But maybe the settlers who'd abandoned it had left something edible behind. A little flour or a few beans in the bottom of a sack, some dry bread in the corner of a cupboard, or even an airtight of tomatoes or peaches or something.

Gathering himself, he sprinted for the soddy.

The door stood ajar. As he jerked it open, its rotting leather hinges gave way. It collapsed with a thud that sent a billow of dust into the air.

Collin ducked back, pressing himself flat against the wall. His gun was cocked in his hand. His breath caught hard in his chest.

The dust settled in silence.

As the first startled moment passed, Collin found the run had done hell to his side. He felt pain through his whole body now. He *had* to rest awhile.

With a hand braced on the doorframe, he peered into the soddy. It was empty. The bare earth floor showed where furniture had stood, but the only thing left was a broken packing crate.

Wearily, he stepped inside and seated himself on the crate. He returned his gun to its holster and scanned the room.

The sod walls had been whitewashed once. Scabs of lime still clung to them. Shreds of oiled paper covered the holes cut for windows. The ragged remains of calico curtains hung over them.

Someone had tried to make a home here. He wondered what had gone wrong and sent them traveling on. Seemed like something always went wrong for a poor man. A damned lot of things had gone wrong for him.

If things had been just a little different, he figured, he'd have been settled in a soddy like this now himself, with Amanda Mae at his side and a brood of younguns to help with the chores. Only, when he'd got home from the war, the Federal government had said a man who'd fought for the Confederacy couldn't homestead the free lands. And by then Amanda Mae was gone, and it hadn't mattered much anyway.

Before the Civil War, it had mattered a lot. He'd been a Missouri farm boy with plans to marry Amanda Mae and someday get a farm of his own. Then the war began, and Mr. Hefferson had started raising a company to fight for Southern rights. He became *Captain* Hefferson, in a fine gray uniform with brass and gilt shining on it, astride a big black stud horse.

The captain made speeches about the war, promising every recruit a uniform, a riding horse, and five dollars in cash money. He'd promised them they'd all be home again in time for harvest.

Collin had figured five dollars and a horse would give a young man a good start in life. Amanda Mae agreed. She swore she'd wait for him. So he kissed her good-bye and marched off with his squirrel rifle on his shoulder.

But three months' enlistment turned into four years. And it seemed to Collin like he'd spent the whole four years trudging through mud and dust without even boots on his feet. He'd slept on the ground with only a tatter of a blanket, stolen clothes off scarecrows and dead men, been sick with fevers and ague and the trots, and been shot and damn near killed. And Captain Hefferson had never come through with the horse or the uniform or the five dollars in cash money.

When the war eventually ended, Collin got home, to discover his folks' place had been burnt out under Order Eleven, and nobody knew where they'd gone to. Everybody knew what had become of Amanda Mae, though. She'd run off with a blue-eyed Yankee officer.

And what had been the good of it all, Collin wondered. He didn't think that in the whole four years he'd done more than a few days of actual fighting. He was sure he'd never succeeded in shooting any Yankees at all. He couldn't see where his presence in the Confederate Army had made one lick of difference to the outcome of the war.

He gave a shake of his head, suddenly aware he'd dozed. And aware that some sound had wakened him. Frowning, he listened.

He caught the soft sounds of a horse's hooves patting the hardpacked ground. There was a faint jangle of chain, and the creak of saddle leather. A horse with a rider on its back.

Danger.

Or maybe delivery.

He got himself to his feet. With the cocked Remington heavy in his hand, he stepped to a window. He peered through a tear in the oiled paper.

The horse was coming toward the house. It was a small, scraggly pony, the kind of ten-dollar Texas cow pony that came uptrail with the longhorns. The saddle on its back was a roping rig hung with huge tapaderos and strung on a breastplate. A grass rope was on the bow, and a war bag behind the cantle. It was a cowboy's outfit. But the old galoot in the saddle didn't look sturdy enough to work cattle.

A poor old husk of a cowpoke, Collin thought. Likely the old feller was drifting from place to place, asking for work and settling for handouts. Looking at him, Collin felt very sad.

The horse stopped.

In a gravel-rough voice, the old galoot called, "Hallo the house!"

Collin eyed the horse. He needed it. If the man on its back had been younger, he wouldn't have hesitated. But he hated to steal from a worn-out old-timer. Only he sure needed that horse.

He told himself that if he left the old man afoot, a posse would sure find the galoot and take him to town and look out for him. In a way, taking the old galoot's horse would be doing him a favor.

Collin called back, "Hallo yourself. Light and come set a spell."

The old galoot grinned. Swinging stiffly out of the saddle, he answered, "Don't mind if I do."

He was bowlegged as a bull pup with the rickets, and not a lot taller. Heading toward the house, he walked with the shamble of a man who'd worked too hard for too many years and taken too many falls.

Collin wondered if it would be safe to hit him over the head with the Remington. A skull that old might crack like an eggshell. He sure didn't want to hurt the old galoot. He only wanted to save his own hide.

As the old-timer neared the soddy, he disappeared from Collin's limited range of vision. Collin moved over to wait beside the open doorway. He held the gun at waist level, hoping just the sight of it would subdue the old galoot.

He waited.

The old man didn't appear. Collin couldn't even hear him coming. He wondered if the old feller might have collapsed out there. Cautiously, he edged his head past the doorjamb for a look. He could see the cow pony standing ground-hitched, head-hung, and hipshot. He didn't see a sign of the old-timer. Puzzled, he took a step through the doorway.

The hefty butt of a Walker Colt cracked down on the back of his head.

Pike stepped away from the wall where he'd flattened himself beside the doorway. His thumb had pulled back the hammer of the big revolver, but he hadn't thought that would be necessary. He'd buffaloed more than one man in his time. He knew just how hard to swing the Walker Colt when he wanted to put a man out for a while without doing any permanent damage. To be sure, he nudged the fallen man with his boot toe. In reply, he got a faint groan. That was all.

Chuckling to himself, Pike thought as how there was many a young rooster as reckoned he could outwit an old fox. And many a young rooster as had lost his tail feathers trying it.

CHAPTER
THREE

Ida Red's earliest memories were of the cotton fields of Alabama. Her favorite memories were of the gambling man who'd taught her a whole new way of life. When he died suddenly, of a bullet, he left her enough money to set up a genteel and very prosperous parlor house. It was rumored that men came from as far away as Omaha just to visit Ida Red's.

Ida herself was a big woman. She stood a good six feet tall in her stockings of pure silk. Her weight was all firm and well placed. She let none of it go to lard. Although she was now past the age most men considered prime, many a man would have offered her any price he could raise. But Ida was a wealthy woman now. The activities she indulged in upstairs were strictly for pleasure, strictly for free, strictly for an elite chosen simply on her whim.

Jack Hollow's deadline was the railroad running straight down Main Street. Ida Red's was on Main, just a few blocks from the courthouse, across the tracks. Her bedroom on the second floor overlooked the street. A private staircase from the bedroom led to a private door in the side alley. A few of Jack Hollow's leading citizens had been invited through that door and up those stairs. So had a few wild cowboys who'd caught Ida's fancy. But only a few. The young men were generally too callow, the old men too weary, to suit her. Nowadays she usually slept alone.

This morning Ida was sitting up in bed with her back against a stack of goosedown pillows and the pink silk top sheet tucked securely over her ample bosom. Her long brown toes stuck out the bottom into the warm square of sunlight that fell through the front window. A tray holding her breakfast spanned her thighs.

She was very comfortable, very contented, today. She knew secrets. She had been smiling to herself the whole time she gazed out the window at the fracas between Stacy Kogh and Weenie Greenwood. When she'd glanced at the bank and seen three men in linen dusters come dashing out, her smile had broadened.

Her thoughts gave her a good appetite. She was buttering a second biscuit when she heard the knock at the door she'd been anticipating.

"Come on in, honey," she called. Her voice was deep and rich, a low contralto. Every trace of Alabama was gone from it. Her gambling man had taught her to enunciate with the finesse of an academy graduate.

The door slammed open. Rowena Greenwood burst into the room in a flurry of tousled curls and tattered petticoats. She had a forlorn, rag-doll look about her as she exploded into tears.

"Oh, Ida!" she wailed. "It's terrible! I can't stand it! I just can't stand it any more!"

34

Ida set down the biscuit and silver butter knife. She took a sip of coffee. Sharply, she said, "Weenie, stop bawling."

Weenie blinked in surprise.

"Weenie, honey," Ida went on. "Don't you try to flimflam old Ida Red with those off-again, on-again tears of yours. She's been too far and seen too much not to know a danced-up drizzle from a real cloud-burst."

"Huh?"

"You know better than to say *huh*, Weenie. It isn't ladylike. And you know better than to try tricking old Ida Red. It isn't smart. This is a business matter, and we'll discuss it in a businesslike manner. Why don't you close that door and sit down? Have a cup of coffee with me, and we'll wait for Stacy to arrive. Then we'll discuss it all together."

Appalled, Weenie turned obediently to shut the door. She couldn't recall a time in her whole life when turning on the tears hadn't gotten her what she wanted. Her parents, her teachers, her friends, the men, all of them always gave in one way or another to her sobbing.

She seated herself in the bedside chair and looked wide-eyed at Ida Red, wondering just how much Ida knew. She had no idea what to do now. The plan was Stacy's from beginning to end. She decided to play it close and wait for Stacy.

Ida rang for her maid and ordered a fresh pot of coffee with two more cups. The maid brought them. She poured a cup for Weenie and left the tray with the pot on the bureau.

Sipping her coffee, Weenie watched Ida and waited and wondered.

At last a knock sounded at the door. Smiling, Ida called, "Come on in, Stacy dear."

Eustacia Kogh hesitated with her hand on the knob. Her forehead furrowed into a frown as she asked herself how Ida knew who was there. Taking a deep breath, she shoved the door open.

"Come in, child," Ida said expansively.

Stacy looked at Weenie. There was an edge of distress in Weenie's eyes, knowledge that Stacy couldn't read. But it told Stacy something was wrong. One glance at Ida confirmed that. Sly smugness and self-satisfaction glinted in Ida's eyes.

"Would you care for some coffee, dear?" Ida asked, gesturing toward the tray.

Nodding abstractly, Stacy poured herself a cup. What did Ida know, she wondered. She'd always been very careful in discussing the plan with Weenie, making sure she couldn't be overheard. She wondered if one of the men had spilled something to Ida. She'd been leery of trusting them in the first place. One was a friend of Weenie's. The other two were friends of his. They were no better than strangers. She remembered her mother's warnings against trusting strange men. Momma was right, she thought as she eyed Ida warily over the rim of her cup.

Ida smiled at the girls. "Now, I believe you two have come to ask me for leaves of absence."

Weenie looked to Stacy for a reply.

Stacy said, "*I* came to tell you I want to quit."

"Me too," Weenie said, in a faint little-girl voice.

"Same thing," Ida said with a shrug. "If you go, you'll be back. If not here, then in some other house. And *that* would be a shame."

It wouldn't happen that way, Stacy thought. Once she had her hands on her share of that bank loot, she intended to stay independent. She'd live her own life her own way, without catering to anyone's whims but her own.

"You are both charming girls," Ida was saying. "Both very good and very popular."

Weenie smiled coyly.

Honest pride gleamed in Ida's eyes as she went on. "And this is the best house in the West. The very best house, with the very best working conditions and clientele. You'd be foolish to give this up for some slovenly cow crib. I'd really hate to see that happen to two nice girls like you."

Stacy had expected Ida to balk at letting them go. She knew of madames who kept their girls in virtual slavery. She'd heard of girls being beaten and disfigured for running away. She didn't think it would come to anything like that with Ida, but she expected a fight. Gathering her courage, she told Ida, "I've worked out every cent of my debt to you. I don't owe you anything. You can't keep me here."

Ida lifted her brows, mocking surprise. "Why, whatever put a notion like that into your head, child? Goodness, old Ida wouldn't stand in your way. I know how it is. I was your age once. I had a man of my own once."

"Man?" Weenie said.

Cautiously, Stacy asked, "You're not going to try to stop us?"

"I like you girls a lot. I'd hate to lose you," Ida told her. "But if I tried to keep you here against your will, you'd be unhappy. In a genteel house like this, it's bad business to keep a girl who's not happy. A girl who isn't enjoying her work isn't a good worker. If a little vacation will make you girls happy, then you go right ahead."

"We want to *quit*," Weenie said.

"You call it whatever you want," Ida answered. "Just remember, there's not one man in a thousand a girl can really trust. When the time comes and those men of yours have run out on you, you send old Ida Red a wire, and she'll send you train fare back to Jack Hollow."

Firmly, Stacy said, "That time isn't going to come."

Ida answered her with a very knowing smile. "Now, as to your wages —"

"I've got over fifty dollars coming," Weenie said.

Stacy said, "I have nearly a hundred."

Ida went on, "For your own protection, I'll hold your money until you get back."

"What!" Stacy glared at her. "You can't do that! That's *our* money!"

"I don't intend to *keep* it, child." Ida's voice was syrup smooth and sweet. "I'll give you each twenty dollars for traveling expenses. That should get you to your men. I'll hold the rest for you. Like a bank, you might say. It'll be here waiting for you when you get back. After all, you don't want those men of yours to get every cent you have, do you?"

Weenie started to protest. Stacy quieted her with a gesture. To hell with it, she thought. There was no point in hassling over a few dollars when they had thousands waiting for them. The important thing was to get out and go meet the men and collect.

"Now, you run along, girls," Ida said. "Get packed and go meet those men of yours. And have fun while you can, because they're bound to leave you broken-hearted and broke before too long."

"Come on," Stacy grumbled at Weenie as she started for the door.

Once they were gone, Ida leaned back into her pillows and smiled broadly to herself. The girls had confirmed her suspicions when they didn't fight for their wages. They were definitely going after money. Big money. She waited long enough for them to get back to their rooms. Then she rang for her maid.

"Find Jacob Worth for me," she told the maid. "Tell him I have a little chore for him. Tell him to get his tail the hell up here."

"Yes'm," the maid answered. She hurried off.

Stacy and Weenie were bright girls, Ida thought as she sipped the last of her breakfast coffee. But they couldn't hold a candle to old Ida Red.

As Tuck Tobin strode toward the county stable, he realized Curly Hobbs had decided to join him. Curly was stretching his legs, hurrying to catch up. Tuck increased his pace. Curly was huffing when he reached Tuck's side.

"I just thought," Curly said, following Tuck into the stable. "Maybe I'd better come along on the posse with you."

"No need," Tuck grunted, heading for the stall where he kept his horse.

"It could be a long hard ride." Curly's tone implied it might be too much for Tuck. "Could be you'll need help."

"I don't expect to." Tuck took a sidelong glance at Curly. He saw the twist of Curly's mouth, the suppressed grin. He understood that Curly didn't really want to join the posse, but only to rile him with hinting around that he was too old to handle the job alone.

"Might be a fight," Curly continued. "You might need somebody quick with a gun."

Tuck snorted. Curly was quick with a gun all right, spinning it road-agent style and rolling it and snapping off hip shots at bottles on a fence. But he'd never been in a spot where a man's life might depend on how he used his gun.

By the time Curly Hobbs came to Jack Hollow, the town was past its wild days. This bank robbery was the biggest thing that had happened since Curly was appointed town marshal. The worst Curly ever dealt with were saloon brawls. He'd never ridden with a posse in his life.

Suddenly Tuck said, "You know, Curly, maybe you're right. Maybe you ought to come along. It might get rough."

Curly sucked in a startled breath. It was obvious he'd never expected Tuck to take up his offer.

"Sure!" he said, but the enthusiasm in his voice sounded forced.

Turning his back to Curly, Tuck pulled his saddle down from the rack. He slung it over his bay's withers and slid it back to smooth the blanket. Reaching under the bay's belly, he caught the front cinch and tugged the latigo through the ring. As he pulled it up, he glanced over his shoulder.

His voice solemn, he told Curly, "You're right. It could get plenty rough. A lot of real badlands out there. Stone dry. We might ride days and nights, thirsty and hungry. Might be, when we catch up, they'll shoot it out with us. A man could get killed."

Curly stepped around to the bay's off side. He leaned his arms on its rump and frowned at Tuck. "You planning to chase them past the county line?"

"If I have to."

"But you haven't got jurisdiction outside of the county."

"The sheriffs around these parts are my friends. I'll telegraph them what's happened. They'll cooperate."

"Maybe you ought to ask them to raise their own posses."

Tuck shook his head as he snugged up the back cinch. "Got to find out which way that bunch went first. Might be we'll catch them before they reach the line."

"Uh huh," Curly grunted, his tone distracted. "You know, Tuck, if you do cross lines, it might be days, maybe weeks, before you get back."

"Might be," Tuck agreed cheerfully.

"Be a bad thing to leave the town with no law at all for a long time like that," Curly said.

With his back to Curly again, Tuck allowed himself a grin as he pulled the halter off the bay and slipped the bit between its teeth. The bridle was a single split ear. He tugged the bay's ear through the slit and draped the reins over its neck. Struggling to keep his face straight, he looked at Curly.

Curly said, "You know, Tuck, I think maybe I'd best stay here. Somebody's got to be here to keep the peace."

"May be," Tuck said.

Curly gave a quick bob of his head, wheeled, and left.

Tuck backed the bay out of its stall and led it onto the street. The posse wasn't ready to ride yet. No one was waiting around the corner in front of the courthouse. Tuck led the bay on past it and down the street to Jones' Mercantile. He carried his saddlebags into the store and stuffed them with supplies. When he'd finished and returned them to his saddle, he led the bay back to the courthouse. There still wasn't anyone waiting to ride out.

He looped his reins over the hitchrail and stood looking down the street.

His thoughts drifted to Ida Red's.

He had a notion to drop in a minute and see how Stacy Kogh and Weenie Greenwood were. He thought he really should have put an end to that fight, no matter whether it was his business or not. Hell, if he'd stopped it, maybe somebody would have noticed trouble at the bank in time to do something about it, and the robbers would all be in the jailhouse instead of loose.

But it was no good thinking a lot of *if*'s. What was done was done, and now he had to ride out after the robbers. And before he left, he wanted to see Stacy Kogh.

Leaving the horse, he walked down to Ida Red's.

It was still morning. Ida's wasn't open for business yet. There was no answer the first time Tuck pulled the bell cord. He pulled it again, hoping someone would come to the door before those cowboys showed up with word they'd found sign.

At last he heard scurrying footsteps. The door opened, and Ida's maid greeted him.

Suddenly he felt awkward. He almost stammered. "Stacy Kogh. She — I mean — there was a fight between Stacy and Weenie. I thought I'd come by and see if they were all right."

The maid's eyes seemed to mock him as she said, "They're all right. You'll have to come back later. We aren't open for business yet. You know that, Sheriff."

"I'm not here on business. I just wanted a word with Stacy."

"A *word?*" She cocked a brow at him.

Did she think the only thing a man wanted with a woman was a place in her bed? Hell, he enjoyed Stacy's company. He'd enjoy it even if he never got to lay a hand on her. He admitted to himself that he was kind of fond of Stacy. Looking down his nose at the maid, he said gruffly, "Tell Miss Kogh that the sheriff would like a word with her, if she doesn't mind."

"Yes, sir." There was still an air of mockery about the maid as she stepped back, ushering him into the entry hall. "You wait in the parlor. I'll go see if she wants to see you."

Tuck went on into the parlor. It was a lushly ornate room, as stylish as the social parlors of Baltimore and Philadelphia. The Brussels carpet underfoot was thick and soft, muffling his footfalls. The chairs were loveseats, built for two. They were deep and overstuffed, covered with plush. Tabourets held shaded lamps that, when lit, glowed dimly. China spittoons were located discreetly in corners, handy but unobtrusive. The upright piano had whale-oil lamps with crystal prisms that danced with light when the piano was played. It was a warm, happy room in the evenings, filled with song and laughter.

Now its quiet emptiness was almost ghostly. A bit depressing.

As Tuck stood waiting, his hat in his hands, he wondered just what he was going to say to Stacy. He tried to frame a few words. Nothing seemed quite right.

Stacy Kogh was in her room, packing, when the maid knocked at her door.

"Yes?" she called impatiently.

The maid answered, "The sheriff's here. He says he wants a word with you."

"The sheriff!" Stacy started, frowning with surprise. Could the plan have gone completely wrong? Could the sheriff have realized she'd had a hand in the robbery?

She felt a cold knot in her stomach as she glanced at herself in the dresser mirror. Her hair was all down loose, and she'd taken off the faint traces of paint she used. She wore only a wrapper. The wrapper was all right. But her face, her hair — could she wile a man looking like this?

"If you don't mind," the maid added.

Stacy caught a breath. Tentatively, she said, "Tell him to come back later."

The maid left.

Stacy stood looking into the mirror. If the law wanted her, the sheriff would insist on seeing her now. If it was personal, he'd agree to come again later.

At last the maid returned. She told Stacy, "He says he can't come back later. He's got to ride with a posse."

"Then he's insisting on seeing me now?"

"No, ma'am. I told him you wouldn't see him now, so he left."

Stacy suddenly felt loose in the joints, as if her bones were coming unhinged. She slumped to sit on the bed, and gave a deep sigh of relief. It was all right. It had been personal. The sheriff wasn't wise to her part in the robbery.

She sat a long moment. Then she looked up at the closed door. That was Tuck Tobin who had gone. Now she was packing to leave. By the time Tuck returned, she'd have gone. She'd never see him again.

She felt an emptiness, something like the terrible feeling she'd had when she was orphaned. A good part of her life had ended then.

The aunt in Asheville who'd taken her in had kept her only a few weeks. Then she'd been shipped off to a ladies' academy. To break her of her wild Indian ways, the aunt had said.

It had been like prison, a prison where she was forced into stays and lace, forced to change her walk and speech and manner. They'd made a new person of her, pushing her old happy self into the ground and burying it as if it were dead.

Now, thinking that she'd never see Tuck Tobin again, she felt as if another good part of her life had been taken from her, killed and buried.

It was a frightening feeling. It meant she cared for Tuck. Cared a lot more than she had ever admitted to herself. That was bad. She couldn't allow herself to care for a man.

She remembered the training she'd received in the ladies' academy. She'd been taught that a woman's rightful place in the world was as a wife, and that her wifely duty to her husband was to serve him, to be docile and obedient, a kind of slavery. The only respectable alternative, it seemed, was to be rich and powerful.

The ladies of the academy would hardly have considered a whorehouse respectable. But Stacy found it a desirable alternative to the slavery of marriage. Still,

46

it too was a kind of slavery. And Stacy wanted freedom. The complete freedom she felt only money could buy. Lots of money.

There would be lots of money waiting for her in Omaha. She'd get it, invest it, have an income that would keep her free. She couldn't let a feeling for Tuck Tobin distract her from that. She had to put him out of her mind once and for all.

Trying hard not to think of him, she returned to her packing.

CHAPTER
FOUR

As Tuck strode out of Ida Red's he was asking himself why the hell he'd thought Stacy Kogh would want to see him anyhow. Just because he thought he'd found a special personal warmth in her didn't mean it was really there. Likely she treated all the men that way. To her, he was probably just another customer.

There were a few possemen waiting in front of the courthouse. He looked resentfully at them. He didn't want to join them. He sure as hell didn't want to stand around jawing with them while he waited for the rest of the bunch to show up. He felt like being alone.

His office was in the jailhouse, a small separate building around the corner from the courthouse. Swinging wide, he circled behind the courthouse quad to avoid the men waiting for him and ducked into the office.

It was a little room, with its only window painted over to above eye level. Even with its lamps lit, it was darkly dismal.

Tuck didn't light a lamp. He sat back in the swivel chair with his feet on the desk. His thoughts were on Stacy Kogh. He felt angry at himself, angry at the awareness that he cared enough for her indifference to bother him so much.

Sudden sounds interrupted his brooding. The hubbub was distant, muffled by the jailhouse walls. He frowned a moment, listening, then swung his feet down from the desk and started out. As he stepped through the doorway, Glenn Hotchkiss came barreling around the corner.

"Tuck, they got one!" Glenn shouted.

"One of the bank robbers?"

"Yeah!"

Stretching out his stride, Tuck hurried on. The crowd was down Main aways, closer to the bank than to the courthouse. It was growing fast. He saw Charlie Willis and Shorty Carlisle dash out of the bank and merge into it.

He caught up and pressed through. In the middle of the mob he found the old-timer he'd sent hunting sign, astride that scrawny Texas cow pony of his. He had a leg hooked over the horn, and was whittling himself a chaw off his plug.

A man afoot leaned against the pony's flank. His hands were tied, and the old-timer's throw rope was looped around his neck, the bitter end tied hard to the saddle horn. Slumping against the horse, he looked as battered and bedraggled as if the old-timer had roped and throwed him before bringing him in.

The old-timer worked his cud and cocked an eye at Tuck. "Well, lawman, I got you one of 'em."

Tuck looked the prisoner down. Noncommittally, he said, "You're sure he's one of them?"

Pike nodded.

"Sheriff," Collin McKay said, his voice weary, his eyes morose. "You got the wrong man."

Tuck turned to glance at the crowd. He picked out Shorty Carlisle and beckoned for him. Charlie Willis followed Shorty over.

"What about it, Shorty?" Tuck asked.

Pursing his lips thoughtfully, Shorty studied the prisoner. He glanced at Charlie Willis, then looked at Collin again.

Collin gave a slow, denying shake of his head.

The old-timer nodded.

Shorty sighed. "I got to be honest, Sheriff. I just ain't sure."

"What!" Charlie grunted.

"Hell," Shorty said. "They had on dusters and bandanas over their faces, and their hats pulled down low. Mostly all I saw was fists full of pistols."

Pike fished into his truck and came up with Collin's Army Remington. Casually, he pointed it into Shorty's face. "Like this?"

Gulping, Shorty nodded. "Don't aim that thing at me."

Pike tilted the muzzle of the gun away.

Charlie Willis said firmly, "He's one of them all right."

"Sheriff," Collin started, "I tell you —"

"Don't tell me anything until I ask," Tuck said.

Charlie glowered at Collin. "Where's the money?"

"I don't know anything about any money," Collin answered.

50

"It'll go easier with you if you cooperate," Charlie told him.

Tuck nodded.

Collin looked from one to the other. He looked as if he were considering cooperating. But he shook his head and repeated, "I don't know anything about any money. You got the wrong man."

"Likely the others got the loot," Pike said. "I left a bunch of rannihans following their sign. Colts and pups. Likely they'll lose it. But maybe you got a blind deef hound dog you could send out as would do the job. They left a trail like a railroad track."

"You know where they cut sign?" Tuck asked.

"Hockett's Creek. North a ways. First sign is a dead horse in the creek," Pike told him.

Turning, Tuck called for Glenn Hotchkiss. "Got that posse ready to ride?"

"Ready and raring," Glenn answered eagerly.

"Get them in their saddles. I'll be with you as soon as I've locked up this one."

Once more, Collin tried. "You've got the wrong man."

"Sure," Tuck said, his voice gentle and sympathetic. He pulled Pike's loop from Collin's neck, then laid a hand on his arm. "Come on. A little rest in jail will do you good. You look worn out."

"I purely am," Collin admitted. He followed docilely at Tuck's side. "Hungry, too. And I'm shot. I hurt like hell. You reckon you could chouse me up a doctor, Sheriff?"

"Sure I can. How come you to get shot?" Tuck made the question sound idly curious, not at all suspicious.

Collin gave him a slaunchwise look. "Some fellers shot me and stole my horse. Three of them. Big ugly fellers."

"Why you reckon they'd do a thing like that?"

"Likely they were those bank robbers you're looking for."

"Likely," Tuck agreed as he opened the jailhouse door. He stopped in his office to collect the cell keys from his desk. Jingling them in his hand, he asked, "What did you say your name was?"

"I don't recollect as how I said," Collin answered.

Tuck looked into his face. "Now that you mention it, I don't recollect so either. You want to tell me now?"

"You're not going to find it on any reward dodgers," Collin said.

It wasn't working, Tuck thought. This man knew the kindly approach, knew the sheriff was trying to ease him off his guard. He was playing the game with Tuck, but he wasn't being deceived by it.

Tuck sighed. He didn't feel like getting tough now. He said, "No, I don't expect I would. I wouldn't expect a man to tell me a name that I'd find on a dodger. But I need some handle to put you in the reports by. I'd sooner you don't tell me Bill Smith. I've had so many Bill Smiths already that the county commissioners are sick of them. Judge Winston says the next Bill Smith I bring up in front of him he'll hang on general principles."

"Then I sure ain't Bill Smith."

"I didn't figure you were. Mister, let's get this over with so you can have that doctor you want and I can get on with catching your friends. Give me a name. A good one."

"How about Collin McKay?"

"That's fine. That'll do just fine. Now, how about telling me where your friends went?"

"What friends?"

"The ones you robbed the bank with."

"Sheriff, I've told you and told you, you've got the wrong man."

"I was hoping you'd tell me something different this time."

Collin gave a shake of his head. It was determined, and a little regretful, as if he wished he could help the sheriff.

Well, that was that, Tuck thought. "All right, mister, I'll get them on my own. And when I do, you'll all hang together. Don't expect any good words to the judge from me."

"Robbing a bank ain't a hanging offense," Collin said.

Tuck grunted. He herded Collin on through a bit of a hallway into the back of the jailhouse. There were three cells, a big one for drunks and rowdies, and two small ones for prisoners charged with serious offenses. Tuck jerked open the door on the nearer small cell.

"Inside."

"You gonna untie my hands?"

"I've got a mind not to. You're a damned stubborn bastard. I'm a damned stubborn bastard too, and I've got a mind to just shut this door on you and forget you."

"Only you ain't gonna," Collin said simply.

With a sigh, Tuck hunted up his clasp knife and cut the piggin string that held Collin's wrists. He shoved Collin into the cell and slammed the door. When he'd turned the key in the lock, he said, "While I'm away there'll be some dumb ass of a temporary deputy in charge of looking after you. He probably will forget about you. So you'd damn well better hope I get back off this hunt soon."

"I'm obliged for your concern, Sheriff," Collin said.

Tuck thought his voice wasn't quite as confident as he'd meant it to be. From inside, that cell wasn't a very nice place. Tuck was certain that, given time, he could break McKay down. But there wasn't time. A posse was waiting.

Maybe the posse would take the other two robbers with the money on them and that would be the end of it.

Tuck put the keys back in the desk and went on around the corner to the courthouse. The posse was mounted up and waiting. As he walked toward them, Tuck wondered who to put in charge of the prisoner. He thought of sticking Curly Hobbs with the job. But chances were Curly really would forget to look after the prisoner. Curly would be too busy campaigning for the sheriff's job to actually do it.

He saw the old-timer with the posse, looking like a propped-up scarecrow on that scrawny pony of his. A game old geezer, he thought, but the old feller had

54

already done a good day's work. He shouldn't be going off for more. Not for something as rough as riding out with a posse.

"Grandpa," Tuck said as he stepped up to Pike. "I got a chore for you."

Pike shifted his cud. He spat and said, "I ain't nobody's grandpa. Not as I know of. Leastways not as I'll admit to. I sure as hell ain't yours."

Around him, possemen chuckled. There was tension in the sound.

Pike grinned at his own joke, and told Tuck, "When you want me, holler for Pike."

"All right, Pike. I need a man for a job, and I think you're the man."

"Job pays money, does it?"

"Dollar a day."

"What's it a job doing?"

"Temporary deputy. Keep watch over the jail, guard the prisoner and see to it he gets fed."

"You mean you want me to stay here while you take this posse out?"

"Somebody's got to stay behind."

Pike looked around at the posse. He looked at Tuck. Doubtfully, he asked, "You think you can handle the hunt without me?"

"We can try. I've had some experience in the line," Tuck said.

"I hope so." Pike nudged his pony a step closer to Tuck. Leaning a hand, palm up, toward Tuck, he said, "Dollar a day. I'd reckon about five days to start with."

"Five days it is." Tuck fished a half eagle out of his pocket and put it into the gnarled hand. "The prisoner's name is Collin McKay. The keys are in my desk. Get him a decent meal and a doctor, will you?"

Pike closed his fingers over the money. He touched his hat brim to Tuck and trotted off.

Mounting up, Tuck glanced at Ida Red's. He was thinking of Stacy Kogh again as he led the posse off toward Hockett's Creek.

The cell Collin McKay found himself in was very small and very dark. The only window was in the hall down at the end. Its light had to filter through the crossed strap-iron bars of the cell door. Not much of it reached Collin.

He turned his back to the door and leaned against it, waiting while his eyes adjusted to the darkness. The cell smelled like a horse stall. And it wasn't much bigger than one.

Hell of a place to lock a man in, he thought. He wondered what a penitentiary cell would be like.

The darkness shaped itself into shadowy forms. Groping, he explored them. There was a bunk along one wall, with a thin blanket folded over it. In the far corner there were two buckets. He supposed the one with the tin ladle in it was meant for drinking water. Both were empty.

Swallowing futilely at the dryness in his throat, he stretched himself out on the bunk. It wasn't as uncomfortable as he'd expected. Or maybe, the way he felt, anything was better than standing up. He hoped the doctor would show soon and prescribe food and water. He was too damned achy and tired and hungry and thirsty to worry much about getting himself out of jail. Maybe that sheriff was right, and the rest would do him good.

He didn't realize he'd dozed until a sound woke him. As he sat up, a key scraped in the lock. The cell door creaked open.

Two men stood outside. One held a lantern and a small satchel. The other, the old galoot who'd captured Collin, held a sawed-off shotgun and wore a broad grin.

Eyeing the gun, Collin decided it was a poor time to try an escape. Besides, he needed the wound in his side patched up and his belly filled. Very tamely, he said, "Morning."

"Ain't morning no more. It's afternoon now," the old galoot answered.

Collin grunted. "You took so damn long coming, I figure it must be morning again."

The old galoot chuckled.

His companion, grim-faced as a hangman, introduced himself as the doctor. He demanded to see the wound and get this business over with. After poking and prodding Collin's side, he washed out the bullet gash, took a couple of stitches, and put on a bandage. Advising Collin to get lots of rest, he snapped his satchel shut and stepped out of the cell.

As the old galoot slammed the door shut, Collin hollered, "What about food?"

Nobody answered him.

Get lots of rest, he thought as he lay back on the bunk. Sure. What else was there to do? He wondered if the old galoot would be the one to bring his meals. He thought maybe when the door was opened again, he could overpower the old feller and make his escape. At least he could try.

He dozed again. When sounds in the hallway woke him, he came alert. On his feet, he waited for the cell door to swing open.

But only a piece of it opened. There was a little door within the big door. He hadn't seen that before. It opened at his feet, a hole just big enough for a food tray or a bucket to be shoved through.

They sure as hell didn't mean to give a man a chance to get out of this place, Collin thought as he saw the napkin-covered tray edged into the cell. He picked it up. It smelled good. That was some consolation.

The old man asked for the water bucket. Collin shoved it through the little door. Another bucket was pushed in, full of fresh water. Then the little door slammed shut and a latch clicked.

And that was that for escape.

Settling himself on the bunk, Collin ate. Once he'd taken the edge off his hunger, his thoughts returned to freedom. How the hell could he get the old galoot to open the door?

In the morning, when his breakfast arrived, Collin tried playing sick. The old galoot only chuckled and accused him of exactly what he had in mind.

By the next day, he was feeling a weary despair. It looked like he'd never get the chance to overpower his guard. He decided he'd have to find some other way out of the cell.

He examined the door thoroughly. Its strap-iron bars were heavy-gauge, its frame solid. The lock and hinges were all on the outside. The openings between the straps weren't even big enough for him to get a hand through. The metal flaked rust when he rubbed it, but he couldn't find one damned weak spot in it.

He turned his attention to the floor. There were no planks to pry up and dig under. The floor was paved with huge sandstone slabs that he couldn't have budged with a prybar.

Standing on the bunk, he tested the ceiling. It was of plank. When he sounded a board with his knuckles, it gave back a discouragingly dull thud. Very thick planks spiked to the beams. With a prybar and a decent place to stand and brace himself, he might have been able to work one loose. Without either, it was impossible.

The walls were brick. At one time they'd been plastered and whitewashed. Most of the whitewash was gone. The plaster was cracked and chipping. In the damp corner behind the buckets he found that large patches of plaster were gone, leaving bare brick. He examined the bricks with his fingertips. The mortar was dry and powdery, too scant on the quicklime. As he rubbed at it, it went to sand.

The hope he felt was a very small one. He had a notion it was damned foolishness to expect to break through a brick wall with only his bare hands. But he could think of nothing else to try. At least this would pass the time while he tried to come up with a good idea.

He shoved the buckets off to the other end of the cell, hunkered, and began rubbing at the mortar. It crumbled slowly. Too slowly. He needed some kind of tool to use on it.

After his next meal, he tried holding back the spoon. The old galoot noticed and told him either he returned it or he didn't get any more food. So he went back to scraping mortar with his fingertips. Then he got served a pork chop. He kept back the bone. The old galoot didn't notice.

The chop bone turned out to be a fine tool. Its end gouged out such a shower of rotten mortar that he began thinking this digging at the wall might actually succeed.

CHAPTER
FIVE

It was raining in Omaha.

It had rained yesterday. It had rained the day before. It had been raining when Stacy and Weenie arrived in town.

Standing at the window of the second-floor hotel room, Stacy gazed at the street. Horses, mules, and oxen struggled to draw their loads through the mud. Drivers cursed and snapped their whips, and cursed again when they had to put their shoulders to their mired wagons. Some gave up, leaving weary teams to rest while they took solace in the saloon across the street from the hotel.

With the window closed, the hotel room was muggy, stinking of stale cigar smoke and mildew. When the window was opened, the room filled with the odor of the stockyards just a block away. It was a grimy room in a grimy building. At first sight of it, the women had been tempted to look elsewhere for lodging. But this was where the men were to meet them. Collin McKay had recommended the place because he knew it and knew no one paid much attention to the comings and goings of its clientele.

Assuring each other it was only for a day, two at the most, Stacy and Weenie moved in. Collin and his friends were supposed to come directly to the hotel with the bank loot. Then they'd divvy up and move on to more suitable quarters.

But four days had passed, and still there was no sign of the men.

Waiting, staring through the window at nothing in particular, Stacy found herself thinking of Tuck Tobin. She told herself she was letting that happen too often. She had to forget him. Think about the money. But where was the money?

Weenie had spread cards on the bed. She sat studying them. Turning up a red ten, she peered nearsightedly at it, then set it on a black jack. She wondered just how often she'd done that in the past four days. The cards were limp, the layout too familiar. She looked up at Stacy. "We could play Seven-Up."

Stacy didn't answer.

"Or Bluff."

Stacy didn't even look at her.

She tried once more. "I'm tired of solitaire. Come on, Stacy, take a hand. It'll help pass the time."

Stacy turned away from the window. "I'm going out."

"It's raining."

"I know it's raining."

"Don't snap my head off. It's not my fault," Weenie whimpered.

62

Stacy sighed. She said, "I can't stand this waiting, not doing anything. God knows what's happened. Maybe they've been captured."

"No!"

"It could happen. We knew that from the start."

Weenie knew it, but she didn't want to admit it. She shook her head.

Stacy picked up her rain cape and flung it over her shoulders. As she set her bonnet on her head, she told Weenie, "I'm going to get a newspaper. I'll see if I can find out anything."

"They can't have been captured," Weenie insisted. "They *can't*."

Stacy walked out. Weenie gazed at the door a moment. She rose to bolt it, then walked to the window.

To her nearsighted eyes, the figures on the street below were fuzzy, but she could tell one from another well enough. A brawny teamster leaning his shoulder against a mired dray caught her attention. She was admiring him when Stacy came into sight below.

Planks had been put in the street for a foot crossing. As Stacy stepped onto one, a man in a yellow slicker appeared. He came from under the awning in front of the saloon and headed after Stacy as if he were following her.

Weenie squinted at his back, thinking he looked familiar. She remembered having seen a man in yellow on the street yesterday when Stacy went out to bring in food. It might have been the same man. He'd looked familiar then. She wondered who he was. And had

Stacy really gone out for a newspaper, or was she meeting the man?

Weenie sighed, thinking it would be nice to meet a man. She wished Collin would arrive. He was a very nice man, one of the nicest she knew.

She was still standing at the window when Stacy reappeared. The man in yellow was still following her. That seemed odd. If they'd had a tryst, they should be together now, or going their separate ways, but not walking one behind the other that way.

She watched Stacy cross the planks back to the hotel. The man returned to the walk in front of the saloon. The walk was covered by a metal awning that cut off Weenie's view of it. But the man didn't disappear under the awning. He stopped and leaned idly against one of its supports. He seemed to be watching the hotel entrance. He looked terribly familiar. She was certain she knew him from somewhere.

Stacy's footsteps sounded in the hallway. Weenie went to the door. She waited for Stacy's voice before she threw the bolt back and swung the door open.

Stacy's skirts were hemmed with mud, and her bonnet was dripping. There was a mud-spattered newspaper in her hand. Grim-faced, she held it toward Weenie. "This week's. It just came out yesterday."

Weenie didn't want the soggy paper close enough to her face to focus on it. She didn't want to touch the messy thing at all. She asked, "What does it say?"

"Your friend, Collin McKay, is in the Jack Hollow jail," Stacy told her. "The others aren't."

"Oh no! Poor Collin! Will they hang him?"

"*The others aren't,*" Stacy repeated.

"They won't hang Collin, will they?"

"To hell with Collin. Don't you understand? They've caught McKay, but the other two escaped. *With the money!*"

Weenie frowned. Slowly, she said, "Then they should be here now."

"But they're not."

"Something must have happened."

"Something's happened all right," Stacy agreed. "They've turned tail on us and taken off with all the money for themselves."

"But — but they're Collin's friends. He said we could trust them."

"Nobody can trust anybody."

"Stacy," Weenie asked, "what will they do to Collin?"

"Try him. Probably send him to prison for a few years. What does it matter?"

"I like him."

"And you trusted him, and look where it's got you."

"Where?"

"Here." Stacy waved a hand at the room.

Weenie looked up at the water-stained ceiling. She supposed Stacy was right. It had been a mistake to trust Collin and those two friends of his. Stacy had warned her time and time again that it was a mistake to trust any man. But Weenie liked men. She just couldn't help trusting one once in a while. And Collin had such soft brown eyes. They made her want to cuddle him. Poor Collin. He didn't deserve to go to prison. He'd only been helping out by robbing the bank. He hadn't hurt anybody or anything like that.

Stacy was saying, "I guess I'd better go wire Ida Red for our return fare."

"Do we have to?"

"We don't have enough money left to pay our own way. And there's no point in it. If Ida's willing, let her pay."

Weenie shook her head. She said, "Do you remember that nice man I met on the train coming here?"

"It seems to me you met every man on that train and you thought they were all nice."

"I mean the one I sat next to. The nice fat man with the shiny bald spot."

"What about him?"

"He lives here in Omaha. He told me to look him up. He gave me his card. I could find him. We don't have to go back to Jack Hollow."

"You think we're going back to Ida Red's with our tails between our legs, and giving up on it all?"

"Aren't we?"

"Oh no! You can bet on that. Just because we're going back doesn't mean we're giving up."

"What does it mean?"

"Your dear Collin McKay is in Jack Hollow. He'll know where those partners of his were headed. If he got out of jail, he'd go after them. He'd lead us to our money."

Weenie's eyes widened. "You mean to deliver Collin out of jail?"

Stacy nodded. "I'll go wire Ida for the money now."

As Stacy started for the door, Weenie remembered the man in yellow. She asked, "Stacy, who's your boyfriend across the street?"

"What?"

"The one who followed you off this morning. Who is he? He looks familiar, but I can't place him."

"There was somebody following me?" Stacy said with a frown.

"A man in a yellow slicker. He followed you off and followed you back again. He was waiting across the street, watching the hotel, when you came in. I thought you knew him."

"Where? Is he still there?" Stacy hurried to look out the window.

Weenie joined her.

The man in yellow was there, lounging against the saloon awning support, looking at the hotel.

"Do you see him?" Weenie asked. "Do you know who he is? I'm sure I've seen him before."

"You sure have," Stacy said. "That's Jacob Worth."

"Jacob? But he was in Jack Hollow when we left."

"He's here now. And I don't think it's any coincidence. I think he's here to spy on us."

"Why would he do that?"

"Because Ida sent him. He's not smart enough to do it on his own. It has to be Ida's work. Remember how easily she let us go? Didn't you think that was odd?"

Weenie shrugged. "Ida's nice. Why should she try to stop us?"

"Forget it." Stacy sighed. "I think I'd better go have a few words with Mr. Jacob Worth."

Jacob Worth had never been to Omaha before. He never wanted to come again. He had a notion the rain wasn't ever going to stop, and the girls weren't ever going to move, and he'd spend the rest of his life standing in front of the saloon waiting for something to happen.

The rain had managed to get in around the collar of his slicker, and the mud had seeped through the seams of his boots. He was damp and tired and bored.

The expense money Ida Red had given him was in his pocket. He had half a mind to spend it on whiskey and women, and report back to Ida Red that he'd lost trail of the girls.

Why the hell not? What business did Ida have sending him on a fool job like this? He'd hired on at her place as a bouncer, not a bloodhound. A bouncer's job was good, just hanging around the house, enjoying himself and occasionally roughing up some rowdy. It was a lot better than standing around in the rain. He was sick of the damned rain.

Why the hell not, he asked himself again.

He was on the verge of giving up his watch, stalking into the saloon and getting himself something to take the damp out of his bones, when he saw Stacy again.

She came out of the hotel, paused, and looked straight at him.

For a long flustered moment he just stood there as Stacy stepped into the mud and started across the street toward him. He decided suddenly that he ought to hide. He started to duck for the saloon.

"Jacob!" Stacy called. "Jacob Worth, you stay where you are! I mean to talk to you!"

There were men on the walk. They heard Stacy shout. They understood it was the man in the yellow slicker she'd called to. A lean cowboy with an amused glint in his eye blocked Jacob's way. "Hold up there, mister. I think the lady wants to talk to you."

Jacob grunted, not sure whether to obey or to knock the cowboy down. Before he could make up his mind, Stacy was there on the walk, confronting him.

"Jacob," she demanded. "Are you following us?"

"No, ma'am," he lied. He remembered his manners and pulled off his hat.

Stacy didn't doubt he was lying. She said, "Did Ida tell you why she wanted us followed?"

He shook his head. He supposed the girls owed Ida money or something like that. It hadn't mattered to him. He was just following orders.

Stacy gave him her intriguing professional smile. Her voice softened. "Can I trust you, Jacob? I mean *really* trust you?"

The cowboy who stood watching grinned. "You can trust *me*, ma'am."

She shot him a quick look that told him to mind his own business. He broadened his grin in reply.

He wasn't the only one standing there enjoying the show. It was certainly no place to hold a serious private discussion. Stacy put a hand on Jacob's arm. He flinched at her touch like a shy horse. She looked into his face. "Jacob, dear, let's go where we can talk."

"Yeah, let's!" the cowboy agreed.

Jacob squared his shoulders and stiffened his spine. He glowered at the cowboy the way he did at rowdies in Ida Red's.

The cowboy appraised Jacob's bulk, gave a small shrug, touched his hat brim to Stacy, and went on his way.

Jacob showed Stacy a smug smile. He was proud of the way he could cow lesser men. Stacy answered him with such a melting look of admiration that he forgot Ida Red altogether. He let Stacy lead him across the street and into the hotel.

As they climbed the stairs, she said, "I really can trust you, can't I, Jacob?"

He nodded, feeling very trustworthy at the moment.

"I think it's only fair for you to know why Ida sent you after us," she told him.

He agreed.

She paused to face him. "Jacob, tell me the truth. Do you really like working for Ida?"

"Sure."

"But she's so unfair to you. You're a very valuable man. If it weren't for you, think of all the trouble we'd have from those terrible roughnecks —" She gave a little shiver, as if the very thought appalled her. "Ida Red's would have been torn to flinders ages ago if it hadn't been for you."

He nodded. He thought Ida never had appreciated just how important he was.

"Ida doesn't pay you what you're worth," Stacy went on. "If she were halfway fair to you, she'd have made you a partner in the business by now."

That was an interesting new idea. Jacob considered it. He'd sure like to own a piece of a house. Then he'd hire somebody else to be bouncer. He'd just hang around and enjoy himself. He grinned at the thought.

Stacy let him contemplate it as she led him to the room. When she knocked and called, Weenie opened the door.

With her sweetest smile, Weenie said, "Hello, Jacob! What a wonderful surprise to see you here!"

"Yes'm," Jacob mumbled, reddening. As much as he admired Stacy, he liked Weenie even more. Just looking at Weenie, and having her look back at him that way, made him feel like the biggest, strongest man in the world.

"Weenie," Stacy said. "I think we've solved our dilemma. I think Jacob's going to help us."

"Oh, Jacob!" Weenie flung her arms around his neck and pressed such a warm kiss on his cheek that he didn't doubt he'd help every way he could.

Unwrapping herself from him, Weenie said, "Here, Jacob, you've got to get out of that awful wet slicker before you catch your death of cold."

She began unbuttoning it for him.

"You see, Jacob," Stacy told him as he stood enjoying Weenie's attentions. "There's a great deal of money. Thousands and thousands of dollars. And we know how to get it."

His eyes widened with interest.

"But we're only women," she continued. "We can't do it alone. We need the help of a man. A real man.

One who's not afraid to buck the tiger and make his fortune."

"It's a gambling game?" he asked.

"In a way. But the odds are all with us. If we can get the right man to help us, it's a sure thing. Are you that man, Jacob?" Stacy said.

Weenie looked hopefully into his face. Her wide china-blue eyes were pleading. Hopeful. Admiring.

He grinned. "I reckon I might be. I sure do reckon so."

Ida Red had been liberal in supplying Jacob with expense money. Stacy calculated there'd be enough to see the plan through. She had Jacob buy three tickets on the cars west.

The tickets took them to Hastings. It was the last stop before Jack Hollow. Once it had been the railhead, but Jack Hollow had taken its trade and glory. Now the few surviving businesses huddled together, surrounded by decaying cattle pens and empty saloons. It was drizzling in Hastings when they arrived.

They stayed only long enough to have a meal and hire a rig. The rig was a surrey with a decent enough trotter between the shafts. With the luggage stowed and Stacy and Weenie settled aboard, Jacob took the reins and headed them west.

He was thinking of the future as he drove. He'd have a parlor house of his own. All the women he could ever use. All the whiskey he could ever drink.

But as the dull drizzle persisted and the day dragged on, his thoughts drifted from the future he planned for himself to the job ahead.

72

They were going to break a prisoner out of the Jack Hollow jail. He'd never done anything like that before. He pondered Tuck Tobin. The whole business could get dangerous. A man might even get himself killed. A whorehouse of his own wouldn't do him a lick of good if he was dead.

The rain finally stopped and the sky cleared, but Jacob's mood didn't. He brooded darkly through the long moonlit night.

What with stops along the way, it was sunup before they reached the old Hockett place. The empty soddy loomed in the dawn light like an abandoned tomb. A feeling of foreboding was misting Jacob's mind as he unloaded the surrey and helped the girls set up their camp inside the soddy. When they were finally ready to bed down, it occurred to him he might share Weenie's quilts. But by then he was completely out of the mood.

CHAPTER
SIX

The morning after the bank robbery, Ida Red slept late. It was midmorning when she came downstairs, wrapped in a blue silk gown, and feeling pleasantly warmed by the dreams she'd enjoyed. She was in the entryway when the doorbell rang. Turning, she opened the door herself.

An old man stood before her, hat in hand. He had obviously come directly from the barbershop. The stubble on his chin was mowed close, his face had been thoroughly scrubbed, and his thin white hair was slicked across his skull. He smelled of soap and bay rum. Ida recognized him as the cowhand who'd captured one of the bank robbers. The cowhand Tuck Tobin had put on as temporary deputy.

She smiled at him. "Good morning, Grandpa. What can I do for you?"

"Name's Pike," he told her. He had a silver dollar in his hand. He gave it a significant flip. "What do you reckon you can do for me?"

Amused, she asked, "You think we've got anything here you can use?"

"Chickee, you'd be surprised." The grin he gave her was even more significant than the flip of the coin.

74

"There isn't any guarantee here," she warned. "If you don't make it, that's your problem. No refunds."

"Never asked for a refund in my life," he said.

Looking him down, she thought he was a game old cock. Little, but wiry. Likely he'd been all man in his prime. She had a feeling none of the young snippets who worked for her would understand. They might even poke fun at him.

"You come along with me, Grandpa," she said gently, taking his arm. "Surprise me."

He chuckled as she led him upstairs.

And he surprised her.

Ida invited Pike to come again. He did, that night. And again the next day. On the day that the sheriff returned to relieve Pike from his duty as deputy, Ida suggested he move his gear up to her room.

The hours Ida kept were a lot different from those a cowhand kept on the trail. Despite the comforts of her bed, Pike found old habits persisted. For one thing, no matter when he fell asleep, he'd wake a little before dawn with the urge to be up and on the move.

Each morning, he'd quietly slip out of bed and take the private stairway down to the street. At the livery stable he'd saddle up his cayuse. He'd ride out for a few hours, then return to town, indulge himself in a visit to the barbershop, and be back between the silk sheets, napping, when Ida awoke.

He and Ida were sharing breakfast from her bedtable when he told her, "Ida, I seen a curious thing this morning."

"What?" she asked idly.

"You recollect that hired man of yours that left town the same day the bank was robbed?" Pike said, eyeing her sideways.

"Jacob Worth?" She was suddenly interested. "What about him?"

"I seen him around sunup."

"Where?"

"Up northwest aways. Seen him and both those girls of yours who took off the same day. They were in a surrey, driving overland, toward the old Hockett place. Good-looking trotting horse between the shafts, but plumb wore out. They'd come a far piece."

Ida pursed her lips. A frown line cut her forehead.

"Up to something, ain't they?" Pike asked.

She nodded.

"And you're up to something, too, ain't you?"

She looked askance at him.

He suggested, "You sent that Jacob Worth feller to trail them two girls."

"You're a sharp old coot," she said.

"I got two eyes and some sense between them."

"You want to use them for me?"

"Tracking?"

She nodded.

"Had a notion of that this morning," he told her. "I followed them a ways. Seen where they set."

"They set?"

"In Hockett's old soddy. Unloaded all their traps and such like they was moving in. From the wore-out look of 'em all, I figure they'll stay set for a while."

76

"Why the Hockett place?" she muttered to herself.

He said, "That's where I caught that bank robber, McKay."

Ida lifted a brow at him.

He shook his head. "No, chickee, that bank loot ain't hid there. You think if it was, I'd of left it lie?"

"How the hell much do you know about all this, you old coot?"

"How much do I have to know to figure out the rest for myself? I know a coyote'll suck eggs if there's eggs around. Maybe thirty thousand dollars' worth."

She eyed him.

"You figure that fight them girls had while the bank was being robbed was sort of on purpose," he said. "You figure the girls run off to meet the robbers. You sent Jacob Worth to follow 'em and let you know where they lit. Now it looks like he's gone and throwed his hand in with the girls."

"Damn you," she said, grinning at him.

He grinned back. "The way I see it, the girls never got together with their bank robbers and never got their hands on the money, else what would they be doing back in these parts."

"So their men ran out on them even before I'd expected," Ida commented.

"And now your hired hand's run out on you. The way I see it, chickee, what you need now is a good dependable man to go follow them all, see where they go and what they're up to."

"A good dependable man like you, old man?"

He nodded.

77

"How do I know you wouldn't run out on me too? The same as Jacob's done?" she asked.

"Old woman," he said sternly. "A lot of these young bucks around here are slavering after you like horny bulls, and they'd be right glad to do chores for you. Only most of 'em would slaver after them young chicks too. Me, now, I'm set and settled and downright sensible. I'm a damn sight more likely to come back and share that loot with you than any of these bull calves. And you know that whether we go partners and divvy up, or I just go on my own, I'm going. Chickee, I'm only just offering to share with you. Understand?"

"You old coot," Ida said affectionately. It wasn't the cash that mattered to her, but the game. She smiled.

"You come back to me, you hear? Whether you get the money or not, you be sure to come back. You hear?"

He dallied awhile longer with her before he went to fetch his horse and ride out to the Hockett place. Before he left, he packed his war bag with jerked meat and tinned peaches, and filled two canteens. It might be a short trail, or a long one. He was a man to be prepared for whatever came.

He rode to Hockett's creek. In the gully near the soddy, he dismounted and ground-hitched his horse. He climbed the bank just far enough to peer over the edge. He had a good view of the house. Settling comfortably on his belly, he watched it.

The surrey was out of sight, probably back in the old barn. The trotting horse was hobbled off aways in the cottonwoods, where it could graze. All was still, and silent, and peaceful.

Eventually Jacob came out and caught the horse. He led it off to the barn. In a while, he emerged, leading it in the shafts of the surrey. Climbing into the rig, he drove off eastward.

That puzzled Pike. Once Jacob was out of sight, he crept to the soddy and peeked through a window. The girls were sound asleep inside. So either Jacob was running out on them, or he'd be back. Whichever, Pike decided the girls would stay put for a while. Mounting up, he followed the surrey's tracks.

With the surrey empty of luggage and no passengers to worry over, Jacob made good time back to Hastings. It was late afternoon when he reached town.

Pike perched himself on a rise just outside of town. From it, he could see down the road. He watched Jacob return the rig to the blacksmith it had been rented from. He saw Jacob disappear into the hotel. When Jacob emerged again, it was to lounge on the gallery and indulge in a cigar. At nightfall, he reentered the hotel.

Pike camped the night on the rise. The next morning, he took up his watch again. At last Jacob appeared. Again he lounged on the gallery. Finally he stirred himself to go to the railroad depot. He lounged there until the westbound train arrived. To Pike's disgust, he boarded the train.

Pike's Texas cow pony was a good sturdy mustang with the ability to sprint like a jackrabbit, turn around in its own tracks, and go on and on at an easy lope until hell grassed over. But, even well fed and well rested, it couldn't keep up with a railroad train in open country. So now Pike decided he'd have to start using his sense as well as his eyes.

Once the train was out of the depot, the station agent left the depot to settle himself in a rocker on the hotel gallery. He was sitting there, working a cud of tobacco, when Pike came riding down the street like a ghost from the town's past.

Pike surveyed the ruins of fine saloons that he'd known in their prime. He'd been prime then himself, randy and snuffy, when he'd driven herds uptrail to Hastings. He felt a sadness for days that were gone forever as he dismounted in front of the hotel. He walked stiffly up the steps to the gallery and paused to look around.

The station agent gave him a sociable nod.

He nodded back and commented, "Town ain't much of what she used to be, is she?"

"No, she ain't," the station agent agreed.

"I reckon I ain't either," Pike allowed. He lowered himself into the rocker at the agent's side.

"Don't reckon none of us are," the agent said. He spat and took himself another chaw, then offered his plug to Pike.

"Don't mind if I do." Pike accepted the plug. He lacked the teeth to bite out his chaw. He drew his Green River knife from its sheath, cut a chaw, then returned the plug.

"Don't see many strangers hereabouts nowadays," the agent said, offering Pike a chance to talk about himself.

Instead, Pike took the opportunity to pursue his quest. "I reckon I'm the first one in a piece of time."

"Funny thing," the agent told him. "You ain't. Fact is, you're the second one today."

"Business picking up a mite, eh? Two strangers in town at once."

"Well, no, not exactly. The other one's gone already."

"Young feller, was he?" Pike asked.

The agent gave him a long look and drawled, "A mite younger than you, I'd allow."

"Likely a hell of a mite younger," Pike said with an amused cackle.

The agent nodded.

"Knew it. These young cubs nowadays are always rushing off somewheres," Pike said. "Always off to the big cities. Chicago or New Orleans or San Francisco or the like."

"This one was going to Jack Hollow," the agent grunted. He made it sound like going to hell.

"Jack Hollow?" Pike put surprise into his voice, as if he couldn't understand why anyone would prefer that town to this one. He figured he ought to keep up the conversation a little longer, or the agent might get suspicious. "I been to Jack Hollow. It ain't so much."

"Damn right it ain't! This here would be a lot more town than Jack Hollow if it hadn't up and failed!" The agent worked his cud and spat angrily.

"It surely would," Pike agreed. He jawed on a bit more about the merits Hastings might have had, then took his leave and headed back the way he'd come.

It was turning night, and drizzling a bit, when the train deposited Jacob Worth in Jack Hollow. He stood on the depot platform watching the cars pull out, steeling himself for the chore at hand. He didn't feel much like facing Ida Red. But he had to do it if he meant to have a share in that big money Stacy and Weenie were after. Taking a deep breath, he stepped down from the platform and walked toward Ida Red's.

Lights glowed softly in Ida Red's parlor. The sound of the piano, and of Ida's deep contralto voice, came through the open windows. Reluctantly, Jacob climbed the stairs to the door.

Ida's wasn't the kind of house where the door stood open to any and all who might want in. It was kept latched. He had to tug the bell cord.

The door opened instantly. Suzy, one of Jacob's favorite girls, faced him. Behind her, in the shadows at the far end of the entryway, a bouncer waited and watched. Both smiled as they recognized Jacob. The bouncer relaxed. Suzy turned on her professional charm. "Why, Jacob, where on earth have you been? We've missed you."

"Off," he answered, and he grinned at her. She sure did admire him, he thought. For the moment, he forgot about Ida Red. He beamed at Suzy. "How you been?"

"Busy," she answered, winking at him.

Significantly, he told her, "I reckon you're gonna stay busy."

She lifted a questioning brow at him.

He nodded. But then he remembered his chore. His grin faded. With a sigh, he said, "Only I got to talk to Ida first. I got some business to settle with her."

"I'll see you later, then." Suzy gestured him through the big arch that separated the entry hall from the parlor.

Girls and customers sat in the parlor, entwined in pairs, listening to the music. Ida stood by the piano, its lamps casting their light on her face from the side and below. As she glanced toward Jacob, the shadows gave her features a diabolical cast. And the heavy foreboding that had troubled Jacob before welled in him again. He wanted to turn and run and get the hell out of the whole affair.

Then Ida finished her song. Her audience clapped. Jacob joined in with a forced heartiness. Ida gave him a curt nod, whispered something to one of the men, excused herself to her audience, and headed toward him.

She led him into her office. It was a small cubby behind the parlor, dominated by a large flat-topped desk. She lit the work lamp and seated herself on the edge of the desk.

Jacob stood, shifting his weight from one foot to the other.

Eyeing him expressionlessly, Ida said, "Tell me what happened."

The story Jacob told her was a good one. Stacy had worked it all out for him, and rehearsed him in it until he had every detail down pat. Up to the point where he'd wired Ida from Omaha to let her know he was on the job, it was pretty much true.

The lie began when he said the girls had taken the train out of Omaha to Chicago, and he'd lost their trail and used up all the expense money trying to find it again. He made a face as forlorn as an old hound when he allowed as how he'd had to give up and come back.

To his great relief, Ida appeared to swallow it all, hooves, hide, and horn. She called him a lot of kinds of stupid and told him he was fired.

The foreboding he'd felt all melted away. He was suddenly exuberant, relieved of his worries. He thought it would all work out just fine and he'd be a rich man with a whorehouse of his own. He remembered Suzy then. Hesitating, he asked Ida if maybe he couldn't visit Suzy awhile.

Ida managed to keep her face straight. Briskly, she demanded cash in advance. Jacob paid her out of the expense money he had left. Once his back was to her, he indulged himself in a very smug grin.

When he was gone, Ida slapped herself on an ample thigh. She leaned her head back and laughed softly but heartily. She fingered the coin Jacob had given her, certain it was her own money. His audacity amazed her. She could have admired him for it, if only he weren't such a damn fool.

She hoped Pike would be back soon. She was eager to share this story with him. She missed the old coot.

Smiling to herself, she returned to the parlor.

★ ★ ★

Tuck Tobin sat in the dreary cubicle of his office. Ever since he'd led his dispirited posse back to town without a hair of the bank robbers, he'd spent most of his time in the office. He'd moved his gear from his boarding house to the sleeping room in the jailhouse, on the pretext of guarding his prisoner. The truth was, he just didn't feel very sociable these days.

Now and then, he wrote a bit on the report he was making out for the county commissioners. Mostly he just sat with his feet on the desk.

Stacy Kogh was gone. She'd left on the train just a few hours after Tuck rode out with the posse. She'd refused to see him. She'd said for him to come back later. But she must have known she was leaving. She must have realized she'd never see him again. He supposed she just hadn't cared. And that hurt.

He tried to take his mind off Stacy. He swung his feet down off the desk and leaned over the penciled notes he'd made for his report. He scowled at them in the dim lamplight, marked out a word, added a line to the notes, then put down the pencil. He read what he'd written and picked up the pencil again.

Curly Hobbs walked in.

"Evening, Tuck," Curly said. He shoved his hat to the back of his head and flashed his toothy grin.

"Evening," Tuck grunted, wishing Curly would go to hell. "What can I do for you?"

"Nothing. I saw your light on and thought I'd drop in for a minute." Curly perched a thigh on the edge of the desk and glanced around the dingy office. "When you reckon the commissioners are gonna build a new jailhouse?"

"They promised to do it last year," Tuck said.

"This one's getting awful old and rickety," Curly commented.

Tuck thought Curly meant that for more than just the building. He grumbled, "It ain't so old."

"It's near falling apart. You recollect how old it is?"

"About the same as the town. Twelve, thirteen years."

Curly rubbed a finger at the cracking plaster on the wall. Dust showered down. He said, "It's wore out. Time it got replaced."

"You figure it's time *I* got replaced too?" Tuck said.

Curly looked at him with those politician eyes, all innocence and regret at having to allow it was so. He said, "You've done a damn fine job as sheriff, Tuck. You've earned a rest. Why don't you just withdraw from the election? Forget it. Take it easy awhile."

Tuck just grunted.

Curly dropped his gaze. As if it pained him to say it, he said, "I'll tell you the truth, Tuck. I've been hearing talk. Folks aren't happy about the way you let those robbers get off with the bank money. They figure you can't cut the mustard any more. Tuck, you're out. Don't go through with it and get yourself disgraced losing the election by a landslide. Withdraw. Retire with dignity and honor while you've got the chance."

Tuck cocked a brow at him. "Running scared, Curly? You figure maybe I can beat you in a fair election?"

"Tuck!" Curly sounded hurt deep. "I — uh — hell, I only been saying this for your own good."

86

"You never said or did a damned thing in your life except it was for Curly Hobbs's good. You go spread your tongue oil somewhere else. If you get my badge, you'll have to do it without any help from me." With that, Tuck bent over his report again, the action a dismissal.

Curly shook his head sadly. He sighed, and left.

Tuck stared at the report, not seeing it. He wondered if Curly was right. Maybe he was getting too old for the job. He *had* lost the robbers. They'd ridden into that herd bedded beyond the Hockett place, stampeded a bunch, and covered their tracks so well that all his hunting couldn't find them again. It had been downright embarrassing bringing the posse back so quick, empty-handed. But there just hadn't been any trail left to follow.

A lot of folk wouldn't understand that. They'd hold it against Tuck that the bank money was lost. They'd figure he'd failed at his job. Maybe he would lose the election.

He wondered if it mattered. He felt like nothing really mattered much now. Not with Stacy Kogh gone forever. He thought of resigning the badge and going to find her. But she didn't want him. She'd made that much clear when she refused to see him before she left.

Forget her, he told himself.

He thought of Collin McKay, sitting in his cell, stubborn as an Arkansas jackrabbit. Tuck had tried everything he knew on McKay. Cajoling hadn't worked. Neither had threats. The last time Tuck questioned McKay, he'd come close to losing his temper and trying his fists.

Dammit, McKay knew where to look for the others. Tuck was sure of it. He figured that, loose, McKay would light a shuck straight after them.

Tuck frowned. Thoughtfully, he tapped the pencil on the desk. After a moment, he put down the pencil and leaned back in his chair. Settling his feet on the desk, he sank deep into contemplation.

There was a way he might recover the loot. It was a long chance. A hell of a long one. But maybe it was worth taking.

CHAPTER
SEVEN

It was a long day for a lot of people.

At twilight, the westbound train pulled out of Jack Hollow. With a weary sigh, the station agent closed the depot and headed for Ida Red's to enjoy a few hours' pleasure before going home.

It was full dark when the last cleaning woman put out the last lamp in the courthouse and headed for the side entrance of the Fair Deal Saloon to have her growler filled before going home.

The moon, almost full, was working its way up through patches of scuddy clouds when Tuck Tobin came out of his office and headed for the blacksmith's stable.

Glenn Hotchkiss had the horse saddled and ready for him when he got there. It was gray, almost white, and in moonlight it would be as visible as a beacon fire. Tuck'd had Glenn file a notch in the shoe of its nigh forehoof. That would leave a distinctive print in firm earth. It should be an easy horse to follow.

Tuck thought of asking Glenn to come along tonight. He decided against it. Glenn was no expert tracker. He might accidentally show himself. One man alone could track secretly. Besides, this was Tuck's own damnfool plan, and if it went wrong he'd bear the whole blame himself. He wouldn't pull anyone else into his troubles.

He led the gray back past the jailhouse and on down the street. It would be too obvious if he left it out in front. He tied it close enough to be sure McKay would see it, yet far enough away for it to look innocent. Coincidental.

Back at the jailhouse, he stood and looked at it. No man would pick a horse that color for a getaway if he had any choice. But Tuck figured McKay wouldn't have a choice. McKay would be in a hurry. Desperate.

If everything went according to plan.

In his office, Tuck lit the lamp and took one more look at the sheathed revolver he was leaving in the desk drawer. He took a drink from the bottle he kept in the drawer, then settled in the chair to kill more time.

He found himself thinking about Stacy Kogh, wondering where she was and what she was doing now. He thought if he lost the next election, he'd go after her. Find her. See her. Let her tell him to his face that she didn't care.

But that was no good.

Hell.

At last he decided it was time to make his move. He took one more drink, then splashed a little whiskey on his shirt front. Returning the bottle to its place, he closed the desk drawer. Keys in hand, he went back to McKay's cell.

Since supper, Collin McKay had been hunkered in the corner of his cell, scraping tediously away at rotten mortar. He was doing better than he'd expected. The brick was laid in hollow-wall construction, inner and outer courses joined by headers. Once he'd gotten a couple of the inside bricks loose, he'd managed to pull more out with his bare hands. Now he was trying to free a brick of the outside wall. He had a notion that if it wasn't any firmer than the inside, he might actually be able to make a hole big enough to squirm through. He thought he might even get it done tonight.

He flinched at a sound.

Someone was coming.

Hurriedly, he crammed loose bricks into place. He slid the last one in as he heard the grating of a key in the cell lock. Flinging himself onto the bunk, he sucked breath and tried to calm the banging of his heart. Dammit, if somebody discovered that hole now, all his work would be gone to waste. And he was so close to busting through —

"Evening, McKay," the sheriff grunted as he stepped into the cell. His voice was harsh and thick, and there was a strong smell of whiskey on him.

Collin sat up and blinked at the glare of the lantern the sheriff carried. He yawned and said, "You ain't by chance got that bottle with you, have you, Sheriff?"

"What bottle?" Tuck said with the exaggerated dignity of a drunk.

"The one you been sucking. Smells like you spilt a mite," Collin answered.

"Are you trying to say I been drinking?" Tuck glowered at him.

"Oh, no, I wouldn't say no such thing, sir!" There was mockery in Collin's voice.

Tuck made a growling noise in his throat. "Damn you, McKay! I got a mind to wring your damned neck!"

"Me? What did I do?"

"You're gonna cost me my job, that's what!" Tuck raised his voice, filling it with anger. "That bastard Hobbs is after my badge, and you're trying to give it to him. Damn you!"

"Me?" Collin widened his eyes, wrinkling his brow in an imitation of distress. The sheriff looked upset enough to piss in his britches. And drunk enough not to know if he did. It was funny. But a little sad, too. He'd felt a kind of respect for this lawman. He was sorry to see him going to hell like this. As he spoke, he almost wished he meant what he was saying. "Anything I can do to help, Sheriff?"

"There damn sure is! You can tell me where those friends of yours were headed with that bank loot!"

"Friends of mine? I told you, Sheriff, you got the wrong man. I ain't got a friend around here, excepting for you."

"Hell," Tuck mumbled morosely. He squinted at Collin. "You sure of that, McKay? You sure you ain't one of them?"

"I'm real positive."

"Uh uh." Tuck shook his head. "No. You're lying to me, McKay. That's what you're doing. You're lying to me."

"Would I lie to you, Sheriff?" Collin said.

"Yeah," Tuck answered through his teeth. "You're lying to me and you're making fun of me. Damn you, McKay!"

He made a move to swing at Collin. He let himself almost drop the lantern. Awkwardly, he caught it. Tautly, drunkenly, he said, "If you'd of helped me, I'd of helped you. But no! You got to be a damn stubborn ass. For all I care, you can rot in this damned jail!"

Wheeling, he stalked out. He slammed the cell door behind him. Still cursing, he strode on into his office. He slammed the door between the office and the cells.

He stopped cursing. He drew a deep breath and sighed, trying to ease the tension in his ribs. He wanted one more drink out of that bottle. But he didn't take it. Putting out the lantern, he left the office.

He walked down to the gray horse, gave it a pat on the withers, then went around the next corner. His own bay was tied there. He checked the rifle in the saddle boot and the lashings on the war bag behind the cantle once more. Finally, he returned to the street and took up a position in a shadowed doorway. Standing, watching the jailhouse from his hiding place, he waited.

The sheriff had slammed the door and stalked off.

Collin sat on the bunk, his knees drawn up, his arms around them. He stared at the door as he listened to the sheriff's mumbled curses. The slam of a second door cut them short. Then, a moment later, he heard the thud that he knew was the outside door being closed hard.

93

He didn't move. Not for a long while. Finally, he got up and nudged the cell door gently. With a creaking of its hinges, it edged open.

He gave a slow shake of his head. He hated to see a good man like the sheriff gone to pieces that way. So damned dumb drunken careless as to leave the cell unlocked like that.

Or was it drunken carelessness?

Collin couldn't help but wonder. Tobin didn't strike him as the kind who'd fall into a bottle that easy.

It might be a trick.

It might not.

A man in Collin's position couldn't be too careful. On the other hand, he couldn't let a good chance slide by either.

Cautiously, he shoved open the cell door. The hinges squealed mercilessly. But the noise brought no reaction.

Taking a deep breath, holding it, he crept to the door that separated the cells from the sheriff's office. It swung open at his touch. He looked into the office.

After days in the unlit cell, his eyes were accustomed to darkness. The thin moonlight that spilled over the painted panes of the window gave the room form for him.

He crossed to the window. The bare panes were above his eye level. Hoisting himself with a knee on the sheriff's desk, he looked out.

He could see the empty street. A ways down it, bright in the moonlight, stood a gray horse, all saddled and ready to go. That was handy. All he'd have to do was run out, jump on it, and ride.

This whole thing was shaping up too easy. He didn't trust it. He didn't think his luck could be turning this sweet so suddenly after being so sour for so long. He wondered if he wouldn't be better off back in his cell, digging his way out with a pork bone.

On the other hand, if the sheriff really was setting up an escape for him, maybe he ought to oblige the poor man and go.

After all, he'd have the advantage of his own suspicions. Maybe the sheriff figured on trailing him to the Bordeaux brothers and the bank money. If so, so what? If he watched his back trail close, he'd find out quick enough whether he was being followed. On his guard, he should be able to lose a tracker. And if he didn't — if he couldn't — then he'd end up back in jail. And that's where he was now, so what did he have to lose by playing the sheriff's game?

Nodding to himself, he began to search the office. As he'd thought he might, he found a gun. It was his own Army Remington, in his own holster, and it lay invitingly in the bottom drawer of the sheriff's desk. That was real thoughtful of the sheriff.

Drawing the gun from the holster, he checked out the cylinder. There were bullets in it, all right. He pried one out and examined it closely by matchlight. There were little nicks at the edge of the brass and the lead, where they met. Bright new nicks.

That was a nasty trick to play on a man, he thought. Leave him a gun loaded with bullets that had the powder dumped out. Suppose he'd fallen for the sheriff's game and gone up against the Bordeaux boys with that gun? He'd have got himself real dead real quick. He reckoned he ought to get even with the sheriff for that.

It'd serve the sheriff right to lose his prisoner.

Returning the gun to the holster, he buckled it on just the way he figured the sheriff wanted him to. He ran his fingertips over the gash Bull Bordeaux's bullet had made in the leather, then tested his sore side with a touch. Not very sore. Healing up right nice. Remembering that close call, he was beginning to feel lucky again. He'd never gotten into trouble but what he'd managed to get out again somehow.

Cheerfully, he checked deeper into the drawer. He found the bottle hidden there. Uncapping it, he took a long drink.

Likely the sheriff was hiding somewhere outside, watching the jailhouse and that gray horse, waiting for him to break and run. Likely the sheriff was stewing in his own juices while he waited. Well, let him stew awhile.

With the bottle in his hand, Collin settled himself in the sheriff's swivel chair. He leaned back and rested his boot heels on the sheriff's desk. The whiskey warmed his gullet, and he was more comfortable than he'd been for days. More confident, too.

As he drank, he thought about the Bordeaux brothers. He was sure they hadn't gone to Omaha to meet the girls. Not after the way they'd done him. Likely Lyle would have hightailed straight to Morrison for that woman of his. Lyle and Bull always stuck together, so Bull would have gone there too. Even if they'd moved on from there, chances were good he could pick up their trail.

All he had to do was get rid of that wiseacre sheriff and get some real bullets for his gun and get after them. And after that thirty thousand dollars. Yeah.

CHAPTER
EIGHT

Jack Hollow lay silent, empty in the moonlight.

Three riders came over a rise and moved slowly toward the railroad depot. They halted in the shadow of the water tank.

Stacy Kogh sat easy in her saddle. She had her long black hair pulled back, topped with a Stetson. She was wearing a boy's calico shirt and Levi's. She felt comfortable astride her mount. This was the first time in years she'd ridden astride, but back home in the North Carolina hills she'd always ridden boy-style. She'd ridden and hunted and played with her Cherokee cousins, as wild as any of them, until she was orphaned and sent away to learn to be a lady.

Now, in the night, stalking, with the prospect of a chase ahead, she felt that old wildness fresh in her blood. She felt alive, truly alive.

Only one thought marred the moment for her. Tuck Tobin. According to Jacob, Tuck was sleeping in the jailhouse these days. That complicated things. Tuck had to be gotten out of the way. But he mustn't be hurt. She insisted to Jacob that Tuck mustn't be hurt.

Hidden in the shadow of the water tank, she went over the plan with Jacob once more, hoping he really understood.

While Stacy and Jacob conferred, Weenie Greenwood squirmed in her saddle. She sat a little to one side, very uncomfortable and completely disgruntled. She had never straddled a horse before in her life. No proper lady would ever do such a thing, and Weenie had been reared a very proper lady.

She had complained bitterly when Jacob showed up with men's saddles on the mounts he'd gotten for them. She'd absolutely refused to slip her slender limbs into britches. So, with her skirts bunched uncomfortably and her thighs already aching, she wriggled in the saddle and silently cursed Jacob and Stacy and this whole business. If it weren't for the money, and for poor Collin locked up in the jailhouse, she'd have walked out on it all.

Despite Stacy's advice and assurances, Jacob was nervous. She'd told him it would be simple. All he had to do was pull his bandana over his face, tug down his hat brim, and act fast when the sheriff answered the door. He was to give Tuck a tap on the head. A tap hard enough to lay him out but not hard enough to break his skull. Stacy was very firm about that. Jacob agreed. He didn't want anybody issuing murder warrants on him. He didn't want them issuing any warrants on him. Stacy had promised that, if he did it all right, Tuck would never get a chance to recognize who did it.

It sounded good. It sounded easy. But Jacob's knees felt mushy as he dismounted. His legs didn't want to work. They were awkward under him. Leaving the girls hidden in the shadow of the water tank, out of sight of the jailhouse, he walked slowly around the end of the platform. He led his horse across Main Street, past the courthouse and around the corner.

He stopped suddenly. There was a saddled horse tied at a hitchrail down the street aways from the jailhouse. A good-looking gray horse. He thought it was the same one Glenn Hotchkiss had bought out of a remuda a few weeks ago.

He wondered what Hotchkiss would be doing in this neighborhood at this hour. Keeping Tuck Tobin company, maybe. But if Hotchkiss was at the jailhouse, he'd have tied his horse right out front, wouldn't he?

Jacob puzzled about it awhile. To be sure, he decided to investigate. He dropped the reins of his own mount loosely over the rail in front of the jail and walked softly up to the window. Rising on his toes, he peeked over the painted panes.

The office was dark.

He stepped to the window of the living quarters, where Tuck Tobin should have been bedded down by now. He looked in. Darkness. He put his ear to the glass. He couldn't hear a thing. He decided no one was in there with the sheriff.

Relieved, he looked at the gray. Who'd left it there, and why? Suddenly he remembered the widow Wilson lived just around the corner. Maybe she had a visitor. One who hadn't wanted to brag by leaving his mount right at her doorstep. Sure. That was it. Jacob chuckled to himself. He was supposed to steal a horse for McKay from the county stable, but here was one already saddled and waiting. A gift from Providence. It would do just fine.

From his hiding place, Tuck Tobin saw the moonlit figure of a man leading a horse around the corner and toward the jailhouse. He scowled, wondering who the hell would be prowling around here at this hour, and hoping whoever it was, he'd get out of the way before McKay made a move.

But the man went directly to the jailhouse. He hitched his horse and peered into one window, then the other.

Tuck hesitated. It looked like Jacob Worth. And it looked like Jacob was looking for him. It might be serious business. In any case, he'd better get Jacob away from there before McKay's escape was ruined. He started toward Jacob at a trot.

He stretched his trot into a run as he saw Jacob draw his pistol and lift it to rap at the door with its butt.

Collin McKay was seated comfortably in the sheriff's chair. The sudden rap at the door startled hell out of him.

Leaping up, he grabbed for the gun on his hip. For an instant he almost darted back into his cell. Then he thought it was probably someone looking for the sheriff. Maybe it was someone who carried a gun with live bullets in it. He sure could use some live bullets.

An empty pistol would work as a threat. Leveling the Remington, he stepped to the door and turned the knob.

Jacob was drawn taut, set to act. He rapped at the door with the butt of his gun, then held it raised, ready to slam it into the man who opened the door.

Suddenly he heard running steps and the jangle of spur chains behind him.

The door opened.

Automatically, Jacob swung. He connected. He heard a grunt, and the thud of someone collapsing on the floor.

"Damn!" a voice behind him shouted. "What the hell are you doing!"

Jacob recognized the voice. It belonged to Tuck Tobin. Wheeling, he lashed out with the revolver.

Tuck Tobin was right behind him, reaching to grab his shoulder. Jacob's knuckles, weighted with the pistol, smashed into Tuck's face.

As the sheriff fell, Jacob was turning. Running. He snatched the reins of his horse, vaulted into the saddle, and slapped hide with his spurs.

Something had gone wrong.

That was bad.

To hell with the money.

To hell with it all.

Racing away from the jailhouse, from the girls, from the whole damned dangerous sour plan, Jacob headed for Omaha.

★　★　★

Pike sat with one leg hooked over his saddle horn and a wad of tobacco working in his jaw. The night air put a dull ache into his bones, but he was enjoying himself too much to pay any attention to it.

All day he'd kept watch on the old Hockett place. He'd seen Jacob Worth show up with three horses, all saddled. He'd watched Jacob and the women pack the saddles for traveling. At nightfall, when they'd ridden off, he'd followed.

To his surprise, they went straight to Jack Hollow.

He found himself a vantage point and watched. When he saw Jacob leave the girls hidden in the shadows to go to the jailhouse, he figured he understood their game. They meant to rescue the prisoner.

But when Jacob knocked at the jailhouse door, a figure that looked like the sheriff came charging down the street. Jacob buffaloed whoever answered the door, then buffaloed the sheriff, and hightailed off in the other direction.

Working his cud, Pike spat and chuckled softly to himself. He was sure Jacob's plan had gone wrong and Jacob had gone for his hole like a scared rabbit. Likely nobody around Jack Hollow would ever see Jacob Worth in these parts again.

Good riddance, he thought.

Lifting rein, he moved his horse off to the side. He stayed out of sight of the girls as he swung a circle. When he turned up a side street toward the jailhouse, he saw the bay horse all outfitted and waiting. The sheriff's horse. So the sheriff had a plan too. Pike could guess what it had been. He turned the corner and glanced at the gray. With a nod to himself, he rode on to the jailhouse. There he dismounted.

He found the sheriff lying on the walk in front of the open door. Hunkering at Tobin's side, Pike looked him over. Out cold, but not damaged. Jacob Worth had a good hand for buffaloing. An expert job.

He turned to the man lying just inside the doorway. It was the bank robber, McKay. He didn't seem damaged either.

Satisfied, rather pleased, Pike returned to the sheriff, caught his bulk under the arms, and dragged. Tobin was a big man, and heavy. Pike was huffing by the time he'd hauled Tobin's limp body through the office and back into the cell Collin McKay had occupied. He unbuckled Tobin's gun belt and carried it back to the office with him. The keys were easy to find. He returned to the cell and locked the door.

He'd noticed the bottle on the desk in the sheriff's office. Seating himself in the sheriff's swivel chair, he picked up the bottle. As he gulped from it, he heard the man on the floor moan. Taking the bottle with him, he hunkered at Collin McKay's side.

With the bottle in one hand and his Walker Colt in the other, he said gently, "Easy now, son."

Collin blinked open his eyes. He scowled at the figure he saw. It was the same scrawny old coot who'd captured him at that soddy. Holding a gun as big as a cannon pointed into his face. He blinked again. He still saw the same thing. He groaned again.

104

"It's all right now, son," Pike told him. "Here, have a drink."

Sitting up slowly, his eyes on the cocked Colt, Collin accepted the bottle. He swallowed from it, gulped, and asked, "What the hell happened?"

"You got buffaloed," Pike said.

"Yeah." Collin had figured out that much for himself.

"You make a habit of it?" Pike asked.

Collin grunted. He remembered opening the door. He recalled seeing something flash toward him in the moonlight and feeling the sudden crash of pain in his head. The pain was still there. He touched his fingertips to the sore spot and gave another groan.

Pike rose to loom over him. Backstepping, Pike lowered the gun and said, "If you're busy escaping jail, don't let me slow you down none."

"Huh?"

"That sheriff, now, he ain't gonna bother you. He's asleep in the back. Locked up in a cell. Not likely nobody'll find him before morning."

"Huh?" Collin repeated. He took another long drag at the bottle. Eyeing Pike warily, he said, "You're the one caught me."

Pike nodded.

"Now you're gonna let me go?" Collin said.

Pike nodded again.

Collin pressed his hand to his throbbing head. He thought he shouldn't have taken that last drink. He felt like he sure needed another drink. This didn't make a damned lick of sense. He mumbled, "Why?"

"Suppose you was offered a fancy reward for a man," Pike said, "and suppose nobody come through with it? How would you feel?"

"Right put out," Collin allowed.

Pike nodded. He said, "If you're going, you'd better get up and get. There's a saddled horse outside, just down a ways, if you want it. Not the cayuse out front. That's mine. The gray down the road. You take it if you want."

Maybe it made sense to the old coot, Collin thought. What the hell. The old coot was right. If he meant to get away, he'd better get at it. He dragged himself to his feet. Still carrying the bottle, he started for the door.

"Hold on a minute," Pike snapped at him.

Collins turned and looked back in question.

Pike gestured with the big gun. He pointed it at the bottle. "I'll take that, if you don't mind."

Collin handed it to him.

As he emptied it, Pike watched Collin stumble down the street to the gray horse, haul himself into the saddle, and ride off. He waited a moment, then holstered the Walker Colt and stepped outside to collect his own mount.

The water tank was at the wrong end of the depot. From its shadow, Stacy and Weenie couldn't see down the street to the jailhouse. But if they moved closer there was too much chance McKay might spot them as he and Jacob rode past. So they waited silently, knowing what should be happening but seeing nothing.

106

Weenie's squirming was making her mount nervous. The horse's fidgeting was making Weenie even more uncomfortable. She didn't think she could stand much more of this.

She broke the silence, whispering, "What on earth is taking Jacob so long?"

"It hasn't been so long," Stacy answered. "He's got to steal a horse for McKay, hasn't he?"

Weenie nodded. She wished he'd hurry up.

Suddenly there was a clatter of hooves, the sound of a horse racing off in the other direction.

Startled, Weenie jerked rein. At the jab of the bit, her mount reared. She grabbed for the saddle horn, but she didn't quite make it. With a squeal, she toppled out of the saddle.

Stacy swung off her horse. Automatically, she grabbed the reins of Weenie's mount before it could bolt. Holding it, she bent over Weenie. Frightened, she asked, "Weenie, are you hurt?"

Weenie moaned as she sat up. She brushed her hand at a wisp of hair that had fallen across her forehead. Her face wrinkled in threat of tears. Snuffling, she considered, then shook her head. She whimpered, "I'm all dirty."

Stacy gave a sigh that was partly relief, partly disgust. She held a hand out to Weenie. Accepting it, Weenie stood up. She brushed at her skirts. "I can't ride like that, Stacy," she said. "I just can't do it."

"Either you ride like that or you don't ride at all," Stacy said. "Do you want to go back to Ida Red's?"

Weenie shook her head.

"Then stop complaining. Here, hold the horses while I go see what's happening." Stacy gave her the reins, then started toward the far end of the platform. She moved cautiously through the shadows until she was in a position to see down the street.

There was a horse in front of the jailhouse, a scrawny-looking little animal. She supposed it was the mount Jacob had stolen for McKay. A poor-looking thing in the moonlight. But she didn't see Jacob's horse at all. Just a pale gray tied aways up the road.

Puzzled, she scowled at the open jailhouse door. She wondered if McKay might have turned on Jacob, grabbed Jacob's horse, and made his getaway in the other direction. That would be bad. Very bad. But it looked like that was what had happened.

She started to turn away, to return to Weenie.

Someone appeared in the doorway. It was Collin McKay. Staggering a bit, he came out. He passed up the mount tied in front of the jail. He went on up the street to the gray. Mounting it, he turned it and started toward her.

She ducked back. Racing to Weenie, she grabbed the reins of her horse and scrambled onto its back. "Quick!" she told Weenie. "Come on!"

McKay rode past the far end of the depot platform at a lope.

"Where's Jacob?" Weenie asked as she struggled to get herself onto her horse.

Stacy shook her head. She didn't know. And there was no time to worry about him. Flicking the rein ends at her horse's flank, she set out after McKay.

108

Weenie wasn't having any luck getting onto her horse. For a moment she stood thinking of giving up. But she couldn't give up. She led the horse to the depot steps, climbed onto the platform, and wriggled onto her saddle.

When she finally caught up with Stacy, she asked breathlessly, "What will we do? We need Jacob, don't we?"

"No." Stacy gave a firm shake of her head. She wondered what had happened to Jacob, but she didn't really care. She didn't doubt she could trail McKay to the money and get it without Jacob's help. She was Indian enough to do it. She said, "We don't need him. We don't need any man."

And suddenly she was thinking of Tuck Tobin again.

CHAPTER
NINE

The first thing Tuck Tobin became aware of was pain. His face hurt. Somebody had hit him. Hard.

He realized he was lying on his back. Not on a bed or bare earth, but on stone. He scraped his fingers over the stone. Slowly he opened his eyes. He found darkness blacker than night. Gazing into it, he searched his memory for understanding.

He'd set up an escape for Collin McKay. Jacob Worth had appeared at a critical moment. Tuck had hurried to stop Jacob from ruining the plan. He'd reached out to grab Jacob's shoulder.

With a groan, he recalled the sight of Jacob's hand, heavy with a pistol in it, ramming towards his face.

What had happened then? Where was he now?

Rolling over, he dragged himself onto his knees. Then his feet. He squinted at the darkness, hunting forms in it. He sniffed the air. It smelled like an outhouse.

It smelled like the jail.

Cautiously, he groped ahead of him. His fingers found the strap-iron bars of the cell door. He shoved. The door was locked.

Of course.

McKay had escaped, all right, but not according to Tuck's plan. No, Jacob Worth had come into it. Jacob had apparently come to deliver McKay from jail himself. And he'd succeeded.

Tuck softly cursed himself. He shouldn't have run out to interrupt Jacob that way. He should have realized what Jacob was up to. He should have thought quicker. Maybe Curly Hobbs was right. Maybe he was getting too old and slow for this job.

Muttering curses, he turned slowly. He stared into the darkness, visualizing the cell. The damned thing was as tight as a bank vault. There wasn't any way out, except through the door. No way to open the door except with a key. No way out until someone found him and let him out. And nobody was likely to do that before morning.

He supposed Jacob and McKay had taken the keys. That would mean he'd have to be sawed out of the cell. Hours wasted. Townsfolk talking. Laughing at him. Curly Hobbs laughing and making hay of the situation.

With a groan, he found the bunk and slumped on it. He was done for in Jack Hollow now. Nothing left but to turn in his badge and ride.

He thought he wouldn't mind so much if it weren't for Curly Hobbs. He'd never realized before just how much he hated Curly.

So he'd lost. He supposed he could stand losing. He could keep his head up and ride out with the whole town laughing at him. But he wished to hell there was some way he could throw a spoke in Curly's wheel before he went.

He felt the need to piss, and somehow that added to his sadness. Wearily, he rose and groped for the back wall of the cell. He knew there was a bucket in the far corner. Running his hand along the wall, he located the corner. He squatted to feel for the bucket.

A whisper of cool air touched his hand.

A small draft was seeping between the bricks into the cell. He frowned at that. Finding the bucket, he shoved it out of his way and leaned close to the wall.

He could smell the little breeze. It was fresh night air coming in from outside. Tracing his hand along the wall, he felt the edges of the bricks. There was no mortar between them.

So McKay had been trying to tunnel out of the cell. With a small vague hope, Tuck wondered just how close he'd come to succeeding. He clawed at the bricks.

One came out. Thrusting his hand into the hole, he pulled out more. They tumbled loose, leaving a hole almost big enough for a man to squirm through. But behind that inner wall there was an outer wall. Another layer of brick.

He nudged the wall. It felt solid. He groped along it. Located the draft of night air. Touched the edges of the bricks. His fingers told him a small strip of mortar had been scraped away. Just enough to let the air through. He pressed hard against the bricks, shoved with all his weight. They didn't budge.

"Goddammit!" he grunted through his teeth. So close. But not close enough. Angrily, he grabbed up a fallen brick and slammed it at the wall.

It rammed through.

Where he'd hit, bricks fell out of the wall and the cool damp night air gushed in.

He rocked back onto his haunches and gave a small sharp bit of a laugh. McKay'd been damned close. The jail wasn't as tight as the county imagined. A man could escape.

He struck again. Drove another brick out of the wall. And another. And more, until he'd opened a hole a slender man could have slipped through.

Sitting back, he caught his breath. Then he rose, used the bucket, and finally returned to banging at the bricks until the hole was large enough for a man his size.

It was still a squeeze. He ripped his shirt as he wriggled through the hole. He didn't notice. He was thinking about McKay, thinking maybe it wasn't too late to pick up the robber's trail. Maybe he could save his plan after all.

He'd show Curly Hobbs.

He got to his feet in the courthouse quad. Across the yard he could see as dark squares the windows of the county stable. He sprinted to one and scrambled through it.

He landed in a stall with a big dark horse. It reared, jerking its halter rope, pawing air in surprise. He ducked the hooves and dashed out of the stall.

All around him, horses stirred restlessly. He wondered if he should grab one of them. Maybe Worth and McKay had found his bay. But the bay was his own mount, with his gun in its saddle boot, and supplies packed behind the cantle.

He raced out of the stable and around the block, down to the side street. To his relief, the bay was still there. Grabbing the reins, he vaulted onto its back and laid spurs to its flanks. He swung it around the corner and up to the jailhouse.

For a moment, clouds scudded across the face of the moon. Then they were past, and Tuck could see hoofprints in the dirt street.

There'd been rain enough during the day to dampen the earth. It took prints well. He could pick out the mingled marks of three horses: a small animal carrying a light weight, a larger horse with a heavier burden, and the notched shoe of the gray.

Jacob Worth was a big man with a good forty pounds on McKay. The gray's prints weren't deep enough for it to be carrying Worth. The small horse's prints weren't deep enough for a man McKay's size to have ridden it. So Tuck figured Jacob had been on the big horse, McKay on the gray, and a small rider or a heavy pack saddle on the small horse.

The big horse — Worth — had headed east. The other two turned west toward the railroad depot. Tuck set out after them.

At the depot, he found the sign of two more horses mingling tracks with the gray. Two horses carrying heavy enough to have small men on their backs.

Tuck's guess was that Jacob had been hired to take part in the rescue. He'd been paid and sent on his way. Then McKay met two friends. Tuck hoped they were the bank robbers. Shorty Carlisle had described the robbers as big men, but in the excitement of the robbery Shorty might easily have been mistaken.

Tuck allowed to himself he could be wrong, but, with luck, he was on the trail of three robbers and a pack horse carrying loot as well as supplies. With luck, he'd drag them all back to Jack Hollow and show Curly Hobbs just who was what.

Eagerly, he set out on the trail.

The moon was bright, and the patches of clouds that dashed across its face made only moments of darkness. The winds gusting off the prairie were filled with wild scents. It was the kind of night that set Pike's blood singing with happy memories.

He'd let McKay get out of sight, and let the two women take off after him. Now Pike followed, riding easy, his pony in a rocking-chair lope.

The damp ground held hoofmarks as easy to read as a stamp-iron brand. Pike noticed the notch in one mount's shoe. Likely that was the gray, the horse intended for McKay's escape. A horse meant to be trailed.

Now and then he glimpsed the women topping a rise ahead of him. For a pair of white women he thought, they were doing right well. They stayed close on McKay's trail, not getting themselves lost. But they let themselves get skylit every time they crossed a high place. That was bad. Pike reckoned if McKay had any kind of eye at all, he'd find out quick enough he was being followed.

He reckoned, too, that whoever had come up on his own trail was rushing a mite too much. For a while he pondered who it might be. He didn't think it was Jacob Worth. From what he'd seen, Jacob had thrown in his hand and got the hell out of the game. Pike didn't figure Jacob for a man who'd come back in now.

That left the sheriff.

Pike had locked him in the calaboose, but it shouldn't take a clever man too long to get himself out of an old cracker bin like that. Not if he was any kind of a man at all.

Pike didn't fancy being in the middle. He'd sooner tag along at drag, let the others play out their hands, then make his move when the right time came.

Reaching the bottom of a deep draw, he turned off the trail. He backtracked until he was well behind the sheriff. Then he swung around and picked up the trail again.

Collin McKay rode due west. Out of earshot of town, he put his mount into a hard run, testing its stride, its speed, its stamina. Satisfied that he had a good horse, he eased the pace.

Riding at a lope, he found himself whistling softly. He grinned at himself. He thought he really should be worried when there was so much going on around him, all aimed at him. There'd been a mess of shenanigans behind his escape from jail, and none were his own. But his headache had waned, the night was beautiful, he had a good horse under him, and he was free. He just couldn't work into the mood for serious worrying. He felt like singing instead.

For the fun of it, he counted off things he should worry about.

First came the Bordeaux brothers. They sure wouldn't be happy to have him catch up with them. Likely they'd try to kill him again. He recalled how Bull had told him he wasn't man enough to stand up for himself. Maybe he wasn't. Maybe when it came to a showdown he'd back water. He didn't know. He wouldn't know until the time came. And if he did back water, likely he'd end up dead.

For another thing, there was that damn strange jail-break. The sheriff had started it, and that old geezer had finished the job. Things had happened in between that made no sense to Collin. Somebody had buffaloed him. He didn't think it was the sheriff or the old geezer. That meant a third person. But who?

He discounted the sheriff as a worry. The old geezer had locked Tobin in the jail. It'd be morning before anyone found him and let him out.

On the other hand, once the sheriff did get out of that cell, he might telegraph all the other lawmen around to keep watch for Collin. That could complicate matters considerably.

The old geezer puzzled Collin.

So did the two people who were on Collin's trail now. He supposed one might be the person who'd buffaloed him. He was sure neither was the old geezer. No, these were greenhorns. They'd let him get several glimpses of them over his shoulder. He figured he really ought to be worried about them.

Then there was the useless gun in his holster. He didn't have a single good round for it. Or even a knife. No weapons at all. He'd have to do something about that as quick as he could.

Finally there was the horse he rode. It was a good sturdy mount that could stretch out and go, but it was the wrong color. If the sheriff sent other lawmen a description of the horse, riding it anywhere near a town would be like waving a flag with his name on it. First chance he got, Collin would have to change mounts.

Glancing back, he caught sight of the greenhorns again. It occurred to him that he might be able to wipe several worries off his list all at once. He could swing back far enough to get behind those two, come up on them, and help himself to their horses. Maybe some guns and ammunition, too.

He nodded in agreement with himself, and scanned the shadows ahead. It didn't take long to find a good gully to sideswing through. When he found it, he turned at a gallop. Keeping to the low places, careful not to skylight himself, he turned again. He backtracked far enough to be certain he was well behind the greenhorns, then sideswung to cut their trail.

He slowed as clouds obscured the moon. Judging he should be near sign, he waited for more moonlight.

As the clouds passed the moon, he glimpsed the two riders. They were ahead of him now, just disappearing down behind a ridge.

He grinned to himself as he set out after them.

CHAPTER
TEN

At first Stacy and Weenie had been able to spot Collin McKay as he topped high places. Then he'd set his horse into a hard run.

Stacy put her mount into a run, trying to keep him in sight. Weenie had trouble with her horse. Stacy had to go back and help her calm the skittery animal. Since then, they hadn't spotted Collin. They had to rely on the tracks the gray left in the dirt.

Stacy rode grimly silent, concentrating on tracking. A little behind her, miserable and morose, Weenie concentrated on managing her horse. Suddenly Stacy slowed. She leaned toward Weenie and whispered. "I think there's someone following us."

"What?" Weenie started to pull rein.

"No!" Stacy warned. "Keep on going. Don't look back. We don't want him to know we've noticed him."

"Who is it?"

"How should I know?"

"Don't snap at me," Weenie snuffled. "It's not my fault."

Stacy held back a sharp answer. She glanced over her shoulder, speculating on the rider she'd glimpsed. She'd barely seen him, just a suggestion of shape and motion. It might not even be a man at all, she told herself. Maybe it was just a stray beef or a loose horse.

"Maybe it's Jacob trying to catch up," Weenie suggested.

"If it were, he'd have done it by now. We're not traveling that fast."

"Maybe it's Tuck Tobin."

Stacy nodded.

"What if it is Tuck?" Weenie asked. "What will we do?"

"We'll do what we have to. No matter who it is, we can't let him follow us. We have to get rid of him."

Weenie winced. "You mean *kill* him?"

For a long moment, Stacy was silent. Finally she said, "It shouldn't come to that. I should be able to shoot his horse. That would stop him without hurting him."

"What if you missed and hit him?" Weenie said. "Or you hit the horse and it fell down on him and hurt him? Even if you didn't mean to, you might kill him."

"Shut up!" Stacy snapped. She gigged her horse into a gallop. She was thinking that she could back out. Give up. Let the money go.

But then where would she go? Back to Ida Red's?

She needed the money to buy her freedom. She had to go through with this, no matter what happened. No matter who got hurt.

They were on a downslope. The ground dropped into shadows, then rose to a crest. She nibbled at her lips as she looked up at the crest. It would command a

120

good view of the slope she'd just ridden down. The man on her trail would follow it down the slope.

"That's the place," she told Weenie, pointing at the crest. "We'll swing around behind that ridge, hide the horses, and climb up afoot."

"You'll shoot him from there?" Weenie said, her voice small and thin.

Grimly, Stacy nodded.

This whole trouble was McKay's fault, she thought as they rode to the back of the ridge. If he and his friends hadn't pulled their double cross, everything would be fine now. She'd have her money. She wouldn't be planning to ambush Tuck Tobin, perhaps kill him.

Damn McKay. Damn them all.

There was good brush on the back of the ridge. Drawing rein, Stacy slid out of her saddle and looped her reins on a bush.

Coming up beside her, Weenie said, "Help me down, please."

Stacy grunted in disgust, feeling that Weenie's helplessness was assumed. A woman could take care of herself, if she were willing to try. Weenie was turning into a damned nuisance. Stacy almost said it out loud. But this whole affair was too complicated now, without getting into an argument with Weenie. Sighing, she offered a hand.

Weenie awkwardly worked herself out of the saddle. Clinging to Stacy's hand, she got to the ground. She straightened her skirts and brushed forlornly at the locks of hair that were straggling out of her coif.

Stacy turned away from her and tugged the carbine from its boot. It was a Spencer, Cavalry issue, a new gun, but she'd sighted it in and gotten the feel of it during the time she and Weenie camped at the old Hockett place. She hadn't lost the skill of her wild days. She had a good eye. She knew she could place her shots. It shouldn't be difficult to shoot a horse from under a man at such an easy range. Injure the horse enough to stop pursuit without injuring the rider at all. She was confident of her ability. Even so, the weapon now felt awkward and uncomfortable in her hands.

Weenie stood a moment, watching Stacy get the gun and start up the ridge. Weenie didn't like this part of it at all. She didn't like guns. But it was a relief to be out of the saddle. Every joint of her body ached. When she set out after Stacy, she walked stiffly, giving a little sigh with each step. She understood now why cowboys were bowlegged. She wondered if hours astride that horse would damage the fine lines of her own legs. That would be terrible. She wished she could rest awhile. Sleep. She almost wished she were back at Ida Red's.

Short of the crest, Stacy gestured and ducked low. Whispering for Weenie to get down, she dropped to the ground and stretched out on her stomach. She squirmed to the crest of the ridge and looked over.

Setting the carbine, she sighted on the slope across the way. For a moment, a cloud covered the moon. The skyglow and patches of stars showed the silhouette of the ridge she aimed at. Then the moon came out again, lighting the face of the slope.

Weenie squatted and touched the ground. It was dirty. She was loath to lie on it. She despised dirt. She felt filthy already. Telling herself a little more dirt wouldn't make any difference, she lowered herself to the ground.

As she stretched out, she found it wasn't so terrible as she'd expected. Lying down was very pleasant. The ground wasn't hard at all. She was more comfortable than she'd been since she first mounted that awful saddle.

Resting her cheek on one arm, she closed her eyes. She was thinking of Tuck Tobin, hoping he wouldn't get hurt. She liked Tuck. Then she was thinking of Collin McKay, hoping he'd appreciate how much she was going through just to get him out of jail and get her share of what he rightfully owed her. She hoped once this was all over she and Collin could be friends again. She liked him a lot.

Smiling to herself, she drifted into dreams.

Stacy heard Weenie's breathing slow into the even murmur of sleep. Damn her, this was no time to fall asleep. Reaching out, Stacy started to shake her awake again. But as her hand touched Weenie's arm, Stacy decided it was better this way. Weenie awake would just be a distraction. And Stacy didn't feel like she could handle a distraction right now.

She looked along the carbine's barrel, waiting for a figure to appear in her sights. She hoped it would be a stray animal.

She felt very alone. Taut as a drawn bow. Almost afraid.

A shadow appeared on the ridge as she gazed at it. A man's head, silhouetted against the sky. His shoulders. His body.

Clouds skipped in front of the moon. Stacy blinked. She could see the vague form of the man, the bulk of his horse, blocking the skyglow.

The carbine was cocked and ready. She drew her bead on the figure. She wished to hell the moon would come out again. Give her a good look at him. A clear shot.

But the darkness hung on. And the rider had topped the ridge. He was starting down. In a moment he'd be lost against it until the moon shone again. That might be too late.

It happened suddenly. She hadn't quite realized she was squeezing the trigger. Startled, she flinched as the gun blasted in her hands. Her eyes slammed shut. The thunder of the shot hammered in her ears, and the bitter stench of powder smoke filled her nostrils as the gun butt bucked into her shoulder. She was coughing, her eyes flooding with tears. In that black moment of eternity, she was afraid she might have killed him. And she understood that Tuck Tobin was far more important to her than she'd ever admitted.

Collin had been pacing the greenhorns, watching for them to skylight themselves ahead of him, while he contemplated the best way of taking them by surprise. He'd just topped a ridge and started down it when something exploded.

His horse winced, shying, bolting. Bent low over its neck, he let it run.

That had been a gunshot. He'd felt the nearness of the slug whining past him. Somebody was trying to kill him.

Why?

There was no time to wonder about it. Whoever had fired that shot would likely want to finish the job. Any moment the moon might come out and make a clean target of him. He thought he'd better lose himself quick.

It would be easier to hide afoot than aboard a horse that practically glittered in the moonlight. Swinging a leg over the gray's rump, he crouched in one stirrup. Ready, he jumped.

He hit ground shoulder first, rolling over, coming up on his hands and knees, scrambling into a patch of brush.

It was a good tumble. He'd jolted a little pain into the half-healed wound in his side, but that was the worst of it. Crouching behind the bush, he peered out. He could see the ridge that had been in front of him when the shot was fired. He figured the ambusher was up there. Likely it had been that pair of greenhorns who tried to kill him. Why? What the hell would they want to shoot him for? Who were they, anyway?

He wondered if they thought they'd succeeded. Maybe. Or maybe they'd come hunting him to be sure. He didn't want to hang around waiting for them. Not while he was unarmed. Dropping onto his belly, he wriggled toward the next clump of brush.

125

The gully was deep enough for its bottom to be shadowed when the moon was out. Cautiously, he worked his way down. In the darkness, he got his feet under him. Crouched low, he ran.

He recollected why he'd backtracked to follow the greenhorns in the first place. They had horses. They had at least one gun, maybe lots of guns. He needed a horse and a gun. He wondered if he could sneak around unseen to the back side of that ridge, maybe come up behind them. His Remington was full of useless bullets, but they might not know that. He could get the drop on them, wave the gun around like it meant something. Maybe. Maybe it was worth a try. Certainly, it was worth getting behind them and having a look at the situation.

He darted for more brush, pausing to catch his breath, then moved on. Hopefully, he worked his way through the brush, toward a gap. He waited until clouds darkened the moon again, then squirmed across the bare gap on his belly. As he scrambled into more brush, the moon bared its face again.

By its light, he could see two horses standing tied. They were partway up the blackslope. Farther up, near the crest, he saw two figures huddled together.

He studied the lay of the land. Then, slowly, he began working his way toward the crest of the ridge.

CHAPTER
ELEVEN

Tuck Tobin was riding at a fast lope, his attention on the trail he followed, when he heard the shot.

Startled, he wheeled his horse, meaning to run for cover. As he did it, he realized the shot hadn't been meant for him, but for something beyond the next ridge.

He laid rein to the bay's neck as he set it into a gallop. Swinging wide, well around the ridge, he aimed to come up to one side of the spot he figured the shot had come from.

Suddenly something bolted out of a draw. It was a pale horse, its saddle empty, its stirrups flapping — the gray horse he'd left for McKay. Had somebody ambushed McKay? Why? Dammit, if McKay was dead, then the whole plan was ruined, the bank money lost.

Gigging the bay, Tuck cut across the runaway's path. As he headed it, the gray pulled up short and reared. Tuck grabbed the trailing reins.

He left the gray tied in the brush.

Upslope, he dismounted. The Winchester in his hand, he crept to the peak of the ridge.

Clouds blotted the moon. When they bared it again, Tuck was looking across a shadowy hollow at another rise. He thought the shot had come from there, or somewhere close by.

He spotted the horses first. There were two of them tied partway up the opposite slope. He saw the people then, two figures huddled together at the crest of the ridge.

One was obviously a woman. In the moonlight, he could see her pale hair and full skirts clearly.

As he watched, the other figure rose to its feet. Silhouetted against the sky, the slender form was distinct. Despite the britches and broad-brimmed hat, this too was obviously a woman.

She pulled off the hat and wiped a hand at her face. The grace of the motion was familiar. So was the arch of her neck as she bowed her head slightly.

The breath locked in Tuck's chest as he thought it looked like Stacy Kogh. That was impossible, he told himself. What the hell would Stacy be doing here in the night like this?

But it *was* Stacy. He felt certain of it.

Motion caught his eye. Something had darted from one shadow to another near the base of the slope.

He gazed at the spot.

He saw a man crouching low, ducking between clumps of brush. A man with something in his hand that looked like a gun.

Tuck jerked the Winchester up to his shoulder. As he sighted along it, he thought suddenly that the man in the shadows might be Collin McKay.

McKay was Tuck's only lead to the bank money. Tuck didn't want to kill him. But he sure as hell couldn't stand by and watch McKay attack the women.

Scrambling back to his horse, Tuck slung himself into the saddle. With a jab of his spurs, he sent the bay racing straight over the ridge and downslope toward the crouching figure.

He saw the man start, spin around, and turn the handgun toward him.

It was McKay.

Tuck hoped to hell that gun was the same useless one he'd left for McKay back at the jail.

He was close now, and closing fast.

Collin thumbed back the hammer and let it drop. It clicked on an empty cartridge. He remembered the rounds were duds. With a curse, he rose to his feet and flung the gun at Tuck. He wheeled and ran.

Tuck touched rein, sideswinging the bay. He was almost on top of Collin. Collin twisted to jump away. He stumbled.

Tuck vaulted from the saddle. Collin threw a hand up in front of his face as he saw Tuck slamming toward him.

They fell together. Tuck grappled with Collin as they tumbled and rolled. For a moment, Collin was on top. Then his back was in the dirt and Tuck was astride his belly, grabbing for his throat.

Flailing, Collin slammed the heel of a hand into Tuck's arm. He rammed his other hand at Tuck's face. His knuckles glanced across Tuck's cheek.

Tuck jerked back his head as the blow slid against his face. He was off balance. Under him, Collin bucked, twisted, tried to jerk free. Tuck got a hand, palm down, on Collin's face. Leaning his weight on it, Tuck got himself onto his knees, astride Collin again.

Squirming, gasping for breath, Collin struggled to pull away from the hand that was smothering him. He got his mouth open and sank his teeth into the flesh at the base of Tuck's thumb.

Flinching at the sudden pain, Tuck lost his grip on Collin's face. He jerked back the bitten hand, fisted it, and drove it at Collin.

Collin caught the blow with an upflung arm. At the same moment, he swung his other hand. The edge of it hit Tuck's neck. The fingers grabbed for Tuck's collar. Caught. Jerked.

Tuck was pulled forward. Collin grabbed at him, catching him, pinning both his arms, holding on like a grizzly.

As his arms locked around Tuck's, Collin rammed a knee up between Tuck's legs. It was an awkward try. It succeeded only in throwing Tuck off balance. Then they were rolling again.

Tuck heard the voice of Stacy Kogh calling his name. Calling frantically. A frightened voice. A voice that cared.

Elated, he wrenched at the arms that gripped him and kicked. He squirmed to shove a fist at Collin's ribs. He couldn't get swinging room. The fist barely nudged into Collin's side. But Collin gave a sharp wince and grunted with pain.

130

Tuck remembered the wound then. McKay had a bullet gash in his side. It was only a slight wound, but it was a sore spot. Tuck shoved his fist at it.

Collin winced. Cursed. His grip weakened.

Tuck jerked against the bear hug. This time, it broke. He pulled free and tumbled away from Collin.

As Tuck broke away, Collin rolled himself over. He got a leg under himself and started to his feet.

Scrambling up, Tuck drove at Collin with both fists.

Collin's side hurt. He staggered as he tried to side-step away. Tuck's knotted fists were darting fast and hard at him. One aimed for his breastbone. It hit high, reeling him back. The other was launched at his face.

Collin ducked his chin as he lashed out at Tuck. Tuck's fist hit his eye. His own fist caught Tuck in the ribs. Then Tuck's knuckles rammed at Collin's bread-basket.

The fist hit, driving pain through Collin like a spike. It slammed the breath and strength out of him. His bones went to dust, his muscles to flab. He felt empty of everything except the hurting.

Dimly, he heard a woman protest. "Stop it! You stop that! Don't you hurt him!"

Collin thought it was Weenie Greenwood's voice. He felt a surge of warm fondness for her. Then something jabbed him in the jaw, and he felt nothing more.

Tuck was on his feet and Weenie Greenwood was tugging at his sleeve, shouting for him to stop.

Stacy Kogh was saying, "Tuck! Oh, God, Tuck!"

131

Tuck's anger blurred as he remembered the girls. He gave a shake of his head, trying to collect himself. Backstepping away from the man he'd downed, he turned toward Stacy.

Her head was bare. The moonlight touched her Cherokee cheeks. Shadows hid her eyes. She stood tall and slim in a thin shirtwaist and britches. Her hands were held out toward him. She seemed unreal there in the moonlight.

But she was real. Very real. Anxiously, he asked, "Stacy, are you all right? I heard a shot!"

"Oh, Tuck!" Suddenly her arms were around his neck. Her body was warm against his, and her cheek, pressing his, was tear-damp. He heard the small soft sobbing of her breath.

He'd never known Stacy Kogh to cry. He held her tightly and touched her hair, stroking it gently. Softly, he said, "It's all right now, Stacy. It's all right."

Then he told her with his lips on hers.

For long moments, nothing existed for Tuck but the woman in his arms, her mouth on his. Nothing mattered but her need for him, and his need for her.

Then he came again to an awareness of the situation, a recollection of Collin McKay and the night, and the two women alone in the empty land.

As Stacy nestled her cheek into the hollow of his neck, he asked her, "What happened? What are you doing out here like this?"

He felt her go tense against him. Felt the moment of hesitation in her. Then she was saying, "I'm so glad to see you, Tuck. I was so frightened. That man. He was following us. I — I thought he — I was so frightened!"

"He shot at you?" Tuck asked.

She gave a small shake of her head. Wisps of her hair brushed his cheek. Her voice quavered as she admitted, "I shot at him. I hoped I could scare him away."

"You didn't." He felt the burning anger at McKay again. He was almost sorry Stacy had missed. Almost sorry McKay wasn't dead. But that wouldn't have been any good. He needed McKay. He had to recover the bank money, to prove himself to the town of Jack Hollow. And to Curly Hobbs.

Easing out of Stacy's arms, he turned to look at McKay.

Weenie was kneeling at the downed man's side, her hand on his forehead. As Tuck turned toward her, she looked up. He could see the shimmer of tears on her cheeks.

"Tuck Tobin, you're mean! You hurt him!"

She said it with such injured childlike innocence that Tuck felt a surge of guilt. He answered defensively, "He was sneaking up behind you. If I hadn't spotted him, God knows what would have happened, what he'd have done to you."

"He wouldn't have hurt us," Weenie protested.

Tuck cocked a brow at her. "Do you know him?"

"He — uh —" Weenie's voice caught in her throat. She gave a small cough. "He's been to visit me. He's nice."

"She thinks anything male is nice," Stacy muttered.

Tuck looked to her. "Do you know him?"

"If he's been to Ida Red's, I may have met him," Stacy said. "I don't know. I don't remember them all."

"Did he visit you in Jack Hollow?" Tuck asked Weenie.

She nodded.

If Weenie had met one robber at Ida Red's, she might have met the others, he thought. He asked, "Was he alone? Was anybody with him?"

Weenie's eyes were wide, her face pale in the moonlight. She glanced from Tuck to Stacy, then faced Tuck again. "I don't know. I don't remember."

"You remembered *him* well enough."

"He was nice."

Stacy asked Tuck, "Why? Who is he?"

"One of the men who robbed the bank. I've been trailing him. I was hoping he'd lead me to the others. And the money."

"Oh."

He glanced at McKay again, then looked out at the ridges. "He wasn't alone when he left Jack Hollow. He had help escaping jail."

"Who?" Stacy asked.

"I figured it was the other robbers. There were four horses —" He stopped short, frowning. "Or were there? You two — Stacy, what the devil are you and Weenie doing out here in the middle of nowhere at night like this?"

Stacy and Weenie exchanged glances. Stacy spoke.

"We were heading west. We didn't like Omaha. We decided to try California."

134

"Going to California? Alone? On horseback?" he said incredulously.

"I'm a mountain girl, Tuck. I've got a lot of Indian in me. I've traveled by horseback and camped out a lot."

"But two women alone? That's dangerous. Damned foolishness."

"I know." She bowed her head, looking ashamed. "We didn't plan to ride the whole way. We came partway by train. We meant to go on by train. We just planned to trail for a few days. Tuck, we were both tired of people. We wanted to get away by ourselves for a while. A horseback trip seemed like a good way to do it."

He nodded, knowing the feeling. Still, it was a foolish thing for them to do. He said, "You shouldn't have tried it alone. If McKay had caught up with you —"

"Collin wouldn't hurt anybody," Weenie said. "He's sweet."

Tuck looked at her curiously. Traveling by horseback and camping out didn't seem like Weenie's style at all. An ugly suspicion stirred itself at the back of his mind. He shoved it away before it could take form, insisting to himself that what Stacy said was the truth, and the whole of it.

"Look, did you two ride through Jack Hollow?" he asked.

Stacy replied with an uncertain nod. With downcast eyes, she said hesitantly, "I was thinking of you, Tuck."

The answer flustered him. He didn't want to chase bank robbers. Not right now. He wanted to lie in the warmth of Stacy's arms. It took effort to keep his thoughts on his job. He said, "Did you ride past the depot? Late in the evening, after the rain was all done?"

"Why?"

"I've been following four sets of tracks. I thought they were all bank robbers. But if two of them were yours —"

"I guess they were," she said.

"McKay must have noticed your trail. He must have been tracking you." Tuck glanced over his shoulder at the night. "But there was a fourth horse. What's become of it?"

"Are you sure there was another one?" Stacy asked.

Puzzled, Tuck shook his head. He'd been mistaken about the sign of two horses. Could he have been wrong about the fourth horse, too? Had it been some rannihan whose trail just happened to coincide with the others?

He said, "I ought to backtrack McKay and see what became of those other hoofprints."

"Now? Do you have to?" Stacy said. Her voice was warm and husky. She brushed a loose strand of hair back from Tuck's forehead. "You look so tired. Can't it wait until morning?"

He was tired. Worn out from that fight. Weary of riding. Weary of worrying about the damned bank loot and his reputation and Curly Hobbs. Now his plan to secretly trail McKay to the loot was ruined. He needed to think. He needed to rest.

He looked into Stacy's face. "I reckon it can wait."

Weenie lay in the moonlight, her quilt wrapped around her. She had squirmed until the earth under her took her shape. Now she was comfortable. But she was worried. Gazing at the woolly bits of cloud that marred a sky full of stars, she sorted her thoughts and hoped it wouldn't rain.

She had dozed while Stacy set up the ambush. The shot had wakened her with such a start that it left her dazed. She'd been befuddled, unable to think straight, as things happened around her.

Tuck Tobin's sudden appearance had really messed up the plans she and Stacy had. But then, so had the fact that Collin McKay had somehow got behind them and Stacy'd taken a shot at him.

Poor Collin. It was mean of Tuck to beat him so, and then leave him trussed up like a chicken for the oven, while Tuck and Stacy sneaked off into the brush together.

Stacy was the one who'd always warned Weenie against getting too involved with men, against trusting them at all. Now it looked like Stacy needed her own advice. During these moments in Tuck's arms, she hadn't been playacting at all. Weenie was sure of that. She'd seen too many women in too many roles. She was aware of the subtle difference between a good show and real affection.

She wondered if the sheriff meant more to Stacy than the money. Maybe Stacy would let the whole plan go to pieces. Maybe she'd decided to stay with Tuck and forget the bank money. And poor Collin. If Stacy chose Tuck, then Collin would get a prison sentence, and Weenie'd get nothing.

Sighing at the thought, Weenie stretched. She ached. She'd ridden on that awful saddle and slept in that awful shack and gone through all sorts of misery to get her share of the loot and get Collin out of jail. She didn't intend to let all that misery go to waste. If Stacy Kogh chose to forget the money for the sheriff, let her. From here on, Rowena Greenwood would take care of herself.

She wriggled out of the quilt. Sighing, she felt her hair. It was a mass of tangles. She combed it out with her fingers and fluffed it. She hoped that, in the moonlight, it wouldn't look too bad. Cautiously, she crept toward the shadow that was Collin McKay.

Collin was bound hand and foot. He lay on his side, his knees drawn up, his chin pulled in. He was snoring softly. As she knelt at his side, Weenie thought tenderly that he looked like a little boy curled in his crib. She touched his cheek gently. The stubble on his jaw prickled her fingers.

In a whisper, she called his name.

He made a mumbling noise.

She put her hand on his shoulder and gave a shake. He grunted then. Opening one eye, he squinted at her.

"Shush," she told him. "Don't say anything. I've got to talk to you."

"Weenie?" he said hoarsely. "Is that you?"

"Yes."

"What the hell are you doing here?"

"Stacy and I were following you."

"You? The greenhorns!" He gave a groan. "Did you take a shot at me?"

"We didn't know it was you."

"But if you were following me, you must have — Oh, hell, Weenie, untie me."

"Collin," she told him sternly, "I'm ashamed of you."

"Untie me, honey. I got to get away from here. From that sheriff." He glanced around. "Where is he? Where's Stacy?"

"In the bush together." Weenie sounded put out.

Collin frowned at her.

In her hurt-little-girl voice, she said, "Why did you and those Bordeaux brother friends of yours double-cross us?"

"I didn't have any part in it," he protested. "Untie me, Weenie. I ache something awful. That sheriff beat hell out of me."

"You were with them," she continued. "You're the one who brought them in on it."

"They crossed me, too. They shot me and ran out on me and left me for the law and took off with the money for themselves. I mean to get them. I want to get you your share. Weenie, *please* untie me."

"Shot you!"

"Uh huh. If you don't believe me, look for yourself."

She shook her head. "Really? Are you telling me the truth, Collin?"

"I swear it. For God's sake, untie me before that damn sheriff shows up."

"Collin, will you promise me you won't run out on me? You'll take me to that money and get it and share it with me?"

"I'll do my damnedest. I swear it. Weenie, untie me quick."

She wanted to believe and trust him. She envied Stacy. She wished she could snuggle into Collin's arms and forget her troubles, let someone else do the worrying for a while.

Sighing wearily at the burden of decision, she reached for the ropes holding Collin's wrists.

CHAPTER
TWELVE

"Damn!" Tuck Tobin breathed between his teeth.

Hunkering, he studied the ground in the long morning light. His bay and the women's mounts had been hobbled at the foot of the slope, where there was some decent graze. Now they were gone. So were Collin McKay and Weenie Greenwood. And the guns.

"I'll get him," Tuck said. "I'll rip out his gizzard and make him eat it raw."

Stacy stood watching him. She held her hat in her hands. Her fingers worked nervously at the brim.

Rising, Tuck faced her. "Weenie *let* him go."

"Are you sure?" she asked.

He nodded.

Softly, she said, "I trusted Weenie."

"*I* trusted *you*," Tuck said.

Stacy's eyes widened. Her face taut, she gazed at him. "What do you mean?"

"Stacy, tell me the truth. Did you decoy me while they got away?"

"Tuck! How can you say such a thing?"

"It's not easy," he admitted. He paused, studying her. He felt like hell accusing her this way. He wondered if he were being a fool. If he were wrong, he might be ruining everything he'd found with her last night. But he had to say it. "It's real odd, you and her being out here and him coming here and then the two of them running off together."

"I — uh — Tuck, do you think that Weenie had it planned? Do you think she led me here on purpose because she meant to meet McKay?"

He gave a bewildered shake of his head. "I don't know what to think."

"You know *I* didn't have a part in it." She came toward him as she spoke. Resting her hands on his shoulders, she looked up into his eyes. "Darling, if I'd been in it with them, I'd have gone with them last night, wouldn't I? I wouldn't be stranded here now with you, would I?"

That made sense, Tuck told himself. Weenie and McKay must have used Stacy without her knowledge.

"Maybe they think they've stranded us," he said. "But they haven't. We've *got* one horse."

"What?"

"I caught McKay's horse last night. I left it tied. I — uh — I forgot about it. I'll take you back to Jack Hollow and —"

"Jack Hollow!" she interrupted. "But what about *them*? They're getting away."

"I know."

"Tuck, you can't just turn around and walk off and let them get away with the bank money!"

"I got to take care of you first. I'll get you back to town. Then I'll head after them."

"No!"

142

He frowned at her, surprised by her intensity.

"We've got to stay after them now," she went on. "We've got to!"

Cocking a brow at her, he asked, "Why?"

"The money —" she started. She hesitated. Her eyes on his seemed unfocused, as if she were looking far past him. "You want to get them, don't you, Tuck?"

"Uh huh."

"What *you* want, *I* want."

Thoughtfully, he told her, "Stacy, honey, there's only one horse. No supplies. I don't even have a gun now. It's badlands ahead of us. Hard traveling. Maybe dangerous. I couldn't drag you along. I can't leave you here alone and afoot. I've got to take you back to Jack Hollow."

"I won't be any trouble to you, Tuck. I promise. I'm light. I wouldn't burden the horse riding double. If we stay on their trail now, we can pick up another horse, guns, supplies, somewhere. I can track. I'm a good shot. I can help you, darling. But if we go all the way back to Jack Hollow now, you may lose them forever."

He knew she was right about that. Even if he turned around to start back the minute he'd got her safely to town, it'd be morning before he could pick up the trail again. McKay and Weenie would be better than a day ahead of him. Likely it would rain and ruin their sign. Likely he'd lose them and have to return to Jack Hollow in disgrace.

But it would be wrong to take a woman along on something like this.

"I couldn't ask you to do it, Stacy," he said.

"You're not asking me, Tuck," she insisted. "I'm asking you. I *want* to go with you. If you make me go back to Jack Hollow, I'll just get a horse and follow you. I won't let you go after them alone. I won't!"

Her eyes pleaded with him. Hot dark eyes melting his determination. Hesitantly, he said, "You're sure?"

"I'm sure!"

There was no arguing with her. Not when her eyes were on his like that, and her mouth inviting him so. He slid his arms around her. Held her. Kissed her.

She was the one who broke the embrace. She looked up at the sky. There were scudding clouds flecking it, threatening rain.

"Tuck," she said. "We've got to get the horse and get after them before we lose the trail."

She was right, he thought sadly. He wanted to stay, to hold her, to love her. But there was no time.

The gray stood where he'd left it tied in the brush. As he and Stacy approached it, it gave a friendly nicker. Tuck untied the reins and held them while Stacy swung into the saddle. He handed them up to her, then stepped up behind her.

While the trail was clear and the ground good, they rode double. Then the rain came. It was a fine drizzle that wasn't washing the trail away, but was obscuring it. Dismounting, Tuck walked ahead, studying the sign. Stacy rode behind him, her own gaze on the ground, searching.

By noon the rain had stopped and the clouds scattered. Stopping to rest, Tuck and Stacy drank from the canteen and nibbled at the small supply of jerky

144

Tuck had packed into the gray's saddlebags for McKay's escape. Then they moved on.

Afoot, Tuck was able to find sign. But it was slow going. Too damned slow. It chafed at him. He wanted to get McKay, get the money, get this whole damned business over with.

Stacy had promised she'd be no trouble. She kept her word. She rode uncomplaining. At times she dismounted and walked along at Tuck's side. She helped him search out the trail. He discovered that she had a good eye for it. Even though he felt guilty about dragging her along, he had to admit to himself he was glad she was with him.

It had to be hard on her, he thought. It was hard on him. He could see the weariness in her face. But when his eyes asked if she wanted to rest, she answered with a smile. She'd go on as long as he kept going.

As the long twilight shadows merged, it became impossible to see hoofmarks in the ground. Until the moon was overhead, it was futile to struggle on. Tuck knew there was a small stream ahead. He led Stacy to its bank and stopped. The horse nosed eagerly into the water. Kneeling together, Tuck and Stacy drank.

"We'll rest here awhile," he told her.

She asked, "And then go on?"

"Likely they'll camp the night," he said. "They don't know we're after them. And they'll be as tired as we are. We might be able to catch up while they're camping."

She nodded in agreement. Rising, she got the canteen and the jerky from the saddlebags. She handed Tuck the meat, then uncapped the canteen to refill it.

"Here, I'll do that. You rest," he said, starting to take the canteen from her.

"No. I'll do it. Why don't you unsaddle the horse and let him graze awhile. He's hungry too."

Tuck went to the horse. He stripped and hobbled it, then came back to Stacy's side. Together, they sat gnawing on the jerky.

It was poor fare for her, he thought. When he'd packed the gear for McKay's escape, he had figured it would be enough to keep McKay going, and as much as the robber deserved. Now he wished he'd been more generous. He kept thinking of hot coffee, fry sizzling in a pan, and hot bread baking in the coals.

He broke the silence suddenly. "I should have taken you back to Jack Hollow."

"Why?" she asked.

"This isn't anything for a woman to be doing."

"I'm all right." There was the sound of a smile in her voice.

"You're tired and you're hungry, and you ought to have better food than this."

"It's good food. It's Indian food, and the Indian in me loves it."

He looked at her curiously. The moon was low on the horizon. She was a dark figure silhouetted against the skyglow. He couldn't see her eyes to read them, but there was a suggestion of enthusiasm in her voice. Under her weariness an eager vitality burned.

146

Incredulously, he said, "You really don't mind it, do you."

"Mind what?"

"The hard going. Being out here in the middle of nowhere, worn out, without a decent meal or a decent bed or anything."

"There are worse things." She sounded like she might have experienced some.

He asked, "What things?"

She hesitated. With a self-conscious bit of a laugh, she said, "Corsets."

"*Corsets?*"

"They're really awful, Tuck. You can't draw a decent breath. You're all pent up, and you feel like the soul's being crushed inside you. I'd almost rather be in a coffin than in a corset."

"But you wear one. In town, whenever you're dressed up, you always wear one."

"I *have* to. A proper lady has to be trussed up in stays and laces, gussied up in feathers and fancies. I don't have any choice. What else can I do?"

He started to speak, but discovered he didn't have an answer.

"There aren't many ways for a woman to earn a living, Tuck," she continued. "Most of them require corsets. But someday I'll be free. I'll get what I want."

"What do you want?"

"I —" She paused. Making a broad sweep of her hand toward the horizon, she said, "This! The land, the sky, freedom."

Tuck looked at the sky, at the vast masses of stars, at the moon lifting itself upward, touching the ridges with silver. He thought he understood. He'd a damn sight sooner be out here like this than at a desk in a dingy office.

"Someday I'll have the money to buy my freedom," Stacy said. She stopped suddenly, in an embarrassed way. With a change of tone, she asked, "What about you, Tuck? What do you want from life?"

He looked at her and wondered. He had always thought she really wanted the life she led, with its fancy finery and ways. He wondered now if she'd settle for a hell of a lot less. He said, "I want you."

For a long moment, she didn't reply. Then she said, "Don't tease me, Tuck. I mean, what is it you want for yourself? Are you happy being sheriff of Jack Hollow?"

"Sure." He said it as if he meant it, but now he wasn't certain. When he'd been a young drover, he'd known he wanted something more than just herding beef. He'd gotten into law work by accident, giving a hand to the town marshal during a brawl, then being offered a job as deputy. He'd taken it. He'd stayed. He'd run for sheriff and been elected. It had all happened to him. He hadn't exactly chosen it. Confronted with the question, he wondered if he was happy this way.

"It's a living," he said. "But I reckon there's a lot about it I don't care for. Too much politicking and writing reports and arguing with the county commissioners. It's kind of — Hell, you know what, Stacy? I'm sick of it. I'm sick of shaking hands and smiling and

148

slick-tonguing folks, trying to keep them liking me when the truth is I don't like them. Sheriffing isn't the kind of a man's job it was when the country was wild. It's got to where it's not fit work for any but the likes of Curly Hobbs."

"Then why do you go on with it? Why don't you quit? Go somewhere else? Do something else?"

He shook his head. He didn't know. Slowly, he allowed, "Maybe I will. Maybe once I've got this bank business cleared up, I'll call it quits." He licked at his lips. Leaned toward her. Peered intently at her moontraced figure. "Stacy, I could raise a stake and get a place on the free range with a few head of stock. I could get a place of my own going. It wouldn't be much, maybe just a lot of hard work and hard times, but it'd be my own. It'd mean freedom. For both of us. If you'd come with me."

She didn't answer. She turned away from him.

He thought he shouldn't have said it. Embarrassed, he pretended a deep yawn, then said, "I reckon we ought to get some sleep."

Collin McKay was pleased when the morning rain began. He hoped it would wipe out his tracks. But the rain didn't fall heard enough or last long enough. And when the sun came out again, it got hot.

The bay he led under an empty saddle was balky, tugging at the reins, annoying him. He thought of turning it loose. But it was Tuck Tobin's horse, and it might head back toward Jack Hollow and Tobin might catch it and set out on it after him. He didn't want

Tobin on his trail. Of all the lawmen Collin had run into, Tobin struck him as the most determined. A man who wouldn't give up easy. Tobin downright scared Collin.

At Collin's side, Weenie rode in weary silence. He thought she needed to rest. He needed rest himself. He knew there was water ahead. A little creek cut through the bottom of a shallow draw. He decided they'd stop there. Let the horses drink. Fill the canteens. Stretch their legs. Then move on. God, he was sick of always moving on.

When they reached the stream, he helped Weenie down, then dropped to his knees in the water. He drank, caught his hands full of water and splashed it into his face, and drank again.

Weenie clutched her skirts with one hand while she dipped her kerchief into the water with the other. She dabbed the damp cloth at the dust on her face. Sighing, she said, "I feel awful."

"You feel awful," Collin grunted. He squinted at her through his right eye. The left, where the sheriff's fist had rammed it, was swollen almost shut, turning a dull purple. "Hell, I'd damn near give my whole share of that bank money for a feather bed and a decent meal in a good hotel."

Concerned, she asked, "Does your eye hurt?"

"My eye and my side and my belly and the whole rest of me. I'm beat up and hungry and tired. Weenie, truth is, I'm wore out. Not good for a lot more. I need rest."

She dipped her kerchief again, then touched it gently to the flesh around his eye. "Poor Collin, does that help?"

He put his hand over hers, holding it and the damp cool cloth against the bruises. "It feels good."

She smiled. "Maybe we should camp here for a while."

He nodded in agreement, then sighed and said, "I don't know. I don't know about that damn sheriff."

"We left him afoot. He couldn't possibly catch up with us."

"No," he allowed. "Not if he's hoofing it. Only maybe he ain't on shank's mare no more. Maybe he's got a horse and he's close behind us."

"That's ridiculous."

"I don't know. He's a damn determined man, Weenie. When I lit out of Jack Hollow he was locked up in his own jailhouse, only he got loose and followed me. And *caught* me. He like to of beat hell out of me last night. I don't want him doing it again. Weenie, if I'd knowed him first, I'd never have touched a hand to that Jack Hollow bank."

"Poor Collin." She gave him a light, quick kiss on the cheek. "We've got to rest sometime. We've got to make camp somewhere. We can't go on riding forever."

He nodded, wondering where and when it would be safe to stop. Never, he thought. Once a man got the law after him, it seemed like no place was ever really safe again. Leastways not with law like Tuck Tobin. Collin wished he'd realized that a long time ago, before he ever got mixed up in bank robbing.

151

He looked off to the west. Pointing, he said, "See them rocks yonder?"

Weenie puckered her forehead with the effort of trying to focus her nearsighted eyes on the distant ridge. The rocks were a blur jutting against the sky.

"From the top of them," he told her, "a man could look out and see anything coming toward him. If we get on over to there, we can take turns resting and keeping watch."

She smiled sweetly at him, relieved to have someone else making the decisions. "Whatever you say, Collin."

He grinned at her. "Well, we'd better fill up the canteens while we got the chance. This is the last water before we reach the hideout."

"What hideout?"

"Place up in the hills, other side of that stretch of badland," he said. He rose stiffly to get the canteens from their saddles. As he returned with them, he went on. "It's where I been heading. I figure maybe the Bordeaux brothers would have stopped there. Maybe they left some sign as will tell us for sure we're on their trail."

There were two canteens each on the women's horses, and two more on the bay he'd taken from the sheriff. He dumped them on the bank of the stream. Hunkering with a grunt, he uncapped one and dunked it. Watching, Weenie imitated him and began filling one.

"It's an old Indian trading post, been deserted for years now," he told her. "Not many folk even know it's there. Got a good sweet-water spring on it. Me and the gang camped there a few times. I reckon the Bordeaux boys would have stopped for water and then gone on to Morrison."

"Who's Morrison?"

"It's a place, a town over the line aways. That's where Lyle Bordeaux has that girl friend of his stowed away. Minnie Evans. You know her?"

Weenie made a scornful mouth as she nodded.

"Lyle likes her a lot," Collin said with a grin.

"If I'd known that, I'd have warned you not to bring him in on this. I'd never trust any man who likes Minnie Evans." She cocked an eye at him. "Do you like her?"

"Hell no!"

"Why'd you choose those Bordeaux brothers for the job?"

"Couldn't get nobody else. I thought they'd be all right. They're mean and ugly, but I never knew them to double-cross nobody before." He paused. "Weenie, I'll tell you the truth. I wasn't sure of myself. I figured it'd take somebody mean and ugly to handle the job. Somebody with more grit than I got. I figured the Bordeaux brothers would do."

"What on earth are you talking about, Collin? You're a better man than both of them added together."

"I don't know," he mumbled. He busied himself with capping the canteen and filling another. He didn't want to think about himself, or what he might fail to do if he caught up with the Bordeaux boys.

Once the canteens were filled and stowed, he gave Weenie a hand up onto her mount. Collecting the reins

153

of the spare horse, he stepped into his own saddle, and they rode on.

After a few minutes, Weenie asked him, "What will you do with your share when we get the money?"

"Buy me a little farm and settle down. Give up bank robbing for good."

She looked askance at him. "Really?"

"It's what I always meant to do. What I always wanted."

"Why haven't you done it already? You've had the money before, haven't you?"

He nodded morosely. "I've had it, only I never managed to hang on to it long enough to get me a place with it."

"What did you do with it?"

"I don't know. Sort of got to drinking and gambling or something. It'd get away from me somehow. Always seemed like there was plenty enough to spare for some fun, and then somehow there just wouldn't be no more left at all."

Weenie nodded, thinking how she'd never managed to save anything from her earnings. She said, "Collin, when we get the money from the Bordeaux boys, do you mean to just take our shares, or take it all?"

"All!" he grunted. "After what they done to us, we don't owe them no part of it."

"A whole thirty thousand dollars, just for the two of us." A little smile shaped itself for her as she thought of all that money.

154

"Might not be that much left, the way them boys spend," Collin warned her. "Besides, there's three of us to divvy between."

"Three?"

"Your friend, Stacy. It was her plan to begin with. She's due a share, ain't she?"

"After the way she took on with Tuck Tobin!"

"You reckon she really mean that?" he asked. "You sure she wasn't just being clever, keeping him from suspicioning her?"

"Oh, she's clever, all right. But she was in earnest, too. I saw, Collin. I know. I can tell when a woman really feels that way about a man. Tuck's as good as got her in the palm of his hand."

Collin cocked a brow at her. "You reckon she'd tell him about us? I mean how we planned the robbery together and all?"

Weenie shook her head. "If she did that, she'd be letting on she had a part in it too. She's too clever to do *that*."

"You don't reckon that damn sheriff is clever enough to figure it out for himself, do you?"

"He's too moon-eyed over Stacy to let himself think anything bad about her."

"I wish he were too damn moon-eyed over her to chase after us," Collin said darkly.

"Maybe he is."

"*Somebody's* after us."

"What!"

"I just seen him. Somebody on a horse over yonder to the right aways. No, don't look. Don't let on we know he's there."

Weenie swallowed hard. Keeping her eyes on the rocks ahead, she asked, "Is it Tuck Tobin?"

"I don't know. Damn if I can see how it could be. Damn if I can see how he got out of that jail in the first place. It's spooky." He drew a weary breath. "Anyway, there's somebody over there, riding nigh even with us and trying to stay out of sight. I only just got a glimpse of him. It might be Tobin. I sure as hell don't know who else it might be."

"Possibly some stranger. Somebody who just happened along," she suggested hopefully.

He nodded. He wasn't sure, and he felt too worn to worry about it.

"What can we do?" Weenie was asking.

"Go on up to them rocks. Set up an ambush. If it's him and he tries sneaking up on me again, I'll be ready for him."

"You'll kill him?"

"I don't know. I never killed nobody. I don't know if I got the grit for it."

"I'd hate to see Tuck get hurt," she admitted.

"I'd hate to see *me* get hurt. If it comes to killing, I reckon I'll have to try." He looked at her. "Weenie, if I ain't up to it and he gets us, you're gonna be in one hell of a mess for helping me the way you done."

"Don't worry about me."

"If it happens, you tell him I got myself loose and dragged you along hostage against your will, you understand?"

"Collin, you're sweet."

He didn't have an answer for that.

156

From the corner of his eye, he watched for the rider he'd glimpsed. He didn't catch another sight of the man, but he was certain someone was there, following them.

When they reached the rocky ridge, they swung wide to cross at its lowest point. On the far side, they swung back to halt on the slope behind the high point of rock.

"You look after the horses," Collin told Weenie as he helped her down. He grabbed the Winchester from its boot and hurried to climb the rocks.

Watching him go, Weenie nibbled at her lip. She hoped he'd be all right, and they'd escape Tuck Tobin. She hoped Tuck wouldn't be hurt. It was all Stacy's fault, she thought. Stacy had gone and fallen for Tuck. And the robbery had been Stacy's idea. If they hadn't tried robbing the bank, they wouldn't be in all this trouble now.

Weary with the burden of her worries, Weenie looked at the horses. They stood with their reins dragging. The bay eyed her. The others nibbled at the sparse grass.

She wasn't sure what Collin wanted her to do about them. She certainly couldn't lift the heavy saddles off their backs. And she didn't know how to put hobbles on them. She'd seen it done, but she'd never paid any attention. Stacy had almost been kicked once putting hobbles on one of them. Weenie certainly didn't want to get kicked. But she didn't want the horses running away, either. And Collin had told her to take care of them.

157

She decided to tie the reins. Then, when Collin came down from his lookout, he could do whatever else had to be done.

There were a few small bushes poking from the rocks. One at a time, she led the horses over and knotted the reins in the branches.

Satisfied, she pulled her bedroll from her saddle, picked a fairly level bit of ground, and spread her quilt. She sat down on it and fingered her tousled hair. Her thoughts went again to Collin. She was terribly sorry she'd gotten him into this mess. After a few moments, she lay back, stretching out on the quilt. A moment later, she was asleep.

Atop the rocks, Collin found himself a vantage point. He looked out at his back trail, then scanned the surrounding land, hunting sight of the strange rider.

After a moment, he yawned and rubbed his face. He was careful not to poke the tender bruised flesh around his eye. That eye was swollen almost useless. The other one was gummy, the eyelid so heavy he could hardly hold it up.

He checked the Winchester. Squirming himself comfortable on his belly, he nosed the rifle out over the rock. He drew a bead on his own back trail. The sights blurred as he looked across them. The trail blurred.

Letting the rifle rest on the rock, he scrubbed his fingers through his hair. Yawned. Nodded. He slumped his face into his hands. For a long moment, he was motionless.

Flinching, he realized he'd dozed. He couldn't let himself do that. Gingerly, he prodded the sore eye, trying to wake himself with pain. He picked up the rifle again, settling it at ready.

He nodded again.

The gun slid out of his hands. His head slumped. He began to snore.

CHAPTER
THIRTEEN

Pike was pretty sure he knew now where McKay and the girl were aimed — up to the ruins of Captain White's trading post. He knew the place. He had wintered there a time or two, back when the buffalo were so thick on the plain that a man could have walked on their backs from the Cimarron to the Yellowstone.

Those had been good times. He'd had a good squaw to warm his wickiup and a good rifle to bring down game. The pot was always full. He chuckled softly at his memories. A damn fine squaw, but nothing compared to Ida Red. Now, there was a real woman. All woman. One hell of a woman.

Then he found himself thinking about the sheriff and that woman of his. It was a shame those two got left behind. He knew the sheriff had tied that gray horse off in the brush. He wondered if the two of them would be game to keep on the trail with nothing but the one mount. It was possible. The sheriff had grit. And that woman seemed to be a damned determined female.

Pike decided not to mingle his own sign with McKay's, just in case. He rode off to the right, picking up some distance, paralleling McKay's trail, staying close enough to get an occasional glimpse of McKay and the girl.

The land here was all familiar to him, filled with good memories of wild young days. He grinned as he recollected hunts and brawls and moonlit nights. Those had been damn fine days.

He roused himself from his reminiscences suddenly. Angry, he told himself he was getting old and careless and likely to lose his scalp. Or at least his quarry. As his mind drifted, the pony had drifted too. He'd got into a position where McKay and the girl could have spotted him. Only for a moment, but one moment's mistake could cost a man everything. When he was young and rash, he'd let foolish mistakes get him into some damn tight scrapes.

He moved along cautiously, swinging around for a glimpse of McKay and the girl. They were riding side by side, leading the extra horse. It looked like they might be auguring something. They didn't seem aware of anything but each other.

Shame about those two, Pike thought. They'd make a nice couple. Only likely they'd both end up in jail. Or dead.

Reining in, Pike let the two of them move on aways. Then he swung left, crossing their trail and riding on well away from it. When he was certain he was beyond their hearing, he swung right again and put his pony into a gallop.

There was a high point of rock ahead, a stony weather-broken ridge piled with tumbled boulders. It would give him as good a view of the surrounding land as could be had in this rough country.

He rode into a draw, then upslope. When he caught sight of the rock ridge again, he saw McKay and the girl. They were crossing a low point of the ridge a little east of the peak. He realized they'd picked the same point of rocks he had. Well, that was natural. It was a good place for a lookout. A good place to camp the night, taking turns at watch. He wondered how good a guard the girl would make. She wasn't cut of the same stuff as the dark-headed one. Pretty bit of fluff, though.

Reining sharply, he swung wide, staying out of sight of the rocks. He thought McKay and the girl had looked plumb wore out. It was getting late. Likely they'd make camp, get themselves some sleep.

Reluctantly, he admitted he needed sleep himself. His joints ached. The thought of Ida Red's silk sheets and soft feather bed stirred a longing in his every bone.

Getting old, he thought sadly. Getting soft. Getting to where he wasn't fit for nothing but town living.

The sun was low and the shadows were long. In the hollows among the rocks, it was night already. Dismounting, Pike led his horse down into one dark hollow. He unsaddled and hobbled it there, and gave it a good handful of parched corn from his wallet to make up for the lack of graze. Leaving the pony contentedly eating, he crept out toward the back side of the rocky point.

He found the girl curled up asleep on her soogan. The horses, still saddled, were tied to nearby bushes. They had already stripped the leaves from the brush.

162

There was nothing else within reach for them to eat. As Pike drew near, they shuffled restlessly and nickered at him.

Upslope, in the last fading light, Pike could see Collin McKay nestled in the rocks, head down, asleep.

It was a poor thing for a man to sleep on watch, Pike thought, but there were times a man couldn't help himself. On the other hand, it was a damned poor man who'd sleep without tending his animals first. There was no excuse for that.

Looking at the tied horses, he had a notion to learn McKay a thing or two.

Careful not to jangle hardware, he unsaddled the horses and dumped the gear on the ground. He pulled the bridle off one horse, tossed it onto the heap, and gave the horse a light slap on the rump. It trotted off, paused to roll, then moved on to hunt graze. As Pike released them, the other horses hurried after it.

The nearest decent graze was nigh a mile away. Pike figured the horses wouldn't stop until they'd reached it. Likely they'd have drifted on a piece more by morning.

Chuckling to himself, he returned to his own pony, gave it another handful of corn, then unrolled his soogan and stretched out for a good night's sleep.

He dreamed of Ida Red and pink silk.

Collin McKay woke suddenly, with the bright morning sun warm on his cheek. He mumbled a curse as he realized he'd been asleep on guard. He had slept through the night. Anxiously, he looked down his back trail. There was no indication that anyone had come near it. The sheriff hadn't caught up. But there was no time to be wasted. Snatching the rifle, he scrambled down the slope.

He found Weenie asleep on her quilt. The horse gear was piled nearby. He glanced around. The horses were out of sight.

Hunkering, he shook Weenie's shoulder. "Wake up. It's morning. We've got to get moving."

She opened her eyes. As she sat up, she squinted nearsightedly at him. "Collin? Morning? Already?"

"Yeah. We got to get moving. Where'd you put the horses?"

Still dazed with sleep, Weenie raised a hand to her hair. She tugged at the tangles, then touched the sleep-puffed flesh under one eye. Tracing her fingertips down her cheek, she felt her sun-chapped lips. "I must look terrible!"

"You're beautiful," Collin said curtly. "Where did you put the horses?"

"I left them tied in the bushes."

He shook his head. "You unsaddled them and hobbled them in the grass somewhere. Didn't you?"

"No. Collin, I don't know how. I just tied them. I didn't unsaddle them."

He gestured at the heaped gear. "*Somebody* did."

"Not me."

"Well, it sure as hell wasn't me." Rising, he looked at the saddles as if they might tell him who'd heaped them there. He said, "Somebody stripped the horses and took them off. If it was a horse thief, he'd of took the

164

gear too. If it was that damn sheriff, he'd of took us prisoner. Weenie, there ain't nobody else."

Plaintively, she asked him, "Are you sure you didn't do it?"

He nodded. But suddenly he wasn't so certain. A man could do things while he was half asleep and not remember them at all when he was awake again. He'd sure as hell been tired enough last night to walk in his sleep.

He was still tired. Tired and hungry. Rubbing at his face, he muttered, "God, I need a cup of coffee."

"There's some in Stacy's saddle pack," Weenie told him.

"Good. You fix it while I find the horses. If there's anything to eat, fix it, too. And make it quick. We got to get moving."

Weenie frowned petulantly at him. "I'm not a cook."

"Hell, neither am I, but I can boil a pot of coffee and open an airtight or fry side meat," he snapped.

She began to snuffle.

With a sigh, he said, "Weenie, I got to find the horses and fetch them back. We got to get moving or we'll end up in jail. But I'm hungry as hell. I'd be awful obliged if you'd fix up something for us to eat. You're hungry too, ain't you?"

Still snuffling, she nodded. In her little-girl voice, she said, "I'll try."

He gave her a bit of a grin. Squatting, he pulled Stacy's pack out of the gear and shoved it toward Weenie. Then he began sorting a bridle out of the tangled mess of straps and reins on the ground.

Suddenly he spat a curse.

"What's the matter?" Weenie asked.

He held up a pair of hobbles. "They're loose! The damn horses are running loose!"

Weenie's eyes widened. Her mouth shaped a small circle. "Oh!"

"And I ain't got a throw rope," he added.

"Oh, Collin! Won't you be able to catch them?"

"Maybe," he said doubtfully.

"You've got to!"

He nodded. He damn sure had to catch their mounts. This was no time, no place, to be afoot. Not with a helpless sort of woman like Weenie to worry over. He had to take care of her. Keep her safe from Tobin.

As he looked at her, he felt an urge to cuddle her and comfort her. With a lot more confidence than he felt, he said, "Don't worry, Weenie. I'll get them. We'll be all right."

She gave him a smile of faith. But as he turned away, her smile faded. She understood. They might be in a very bad spot. And there wasn't a thing she could do to help. Except make him that coffee. She'd never done it before. But she'd do it now. Somehow. For him.

Determined, she sorted the pot and a bag of coffee beans out of the gear. She looked at them helplessly. She didn't know what to do next.

She considered for a long while before she finally spoke up. In a very small voice, she said, "Collin?"

166

He'd gotten a couple of bridles untangled, and was tugging the third one free of the gear. He looked up at her in question.

Apologetically, she asked, "How do I do this?"

He swallowed back an impatient curse. Setting the bridles aside, he got a fire started, then got the coffee on to boil. Glancing at the food stores, he saw canned goods. He told Weenie, "Don't worry about the food. We'll eat it straight out the airtights."

She smiled appreciatively at him. "Collin, you're sweet."

He grinned at her, wishing there were time to take her, to hold her. But there was no time. Collecting the bridles, he assured her he'd be back soon with their mounts. He slung the bridles over his shoulder and set out.

He was no expert tracker, but the horses had left clear enough sign for him to follow. He walked along slowly, watching for hoofmarks and droppings. One eye was still swollen. The other blurred whenever he blinked. He longed for that coffee. He felt like hell.

Across a low ridge, out of Weenie's sight, he stopped. Sitting down on a rock, he sank his head into his hands. He wondered if the bank money was really worth all he was going through to get it. Hell, it might be easier than this to work for a living. Even herding cattle couldn't be any worse than this. A dollar a day and found wasn't much of a wage, but at least a working man got to eat regular and wasn't always looking over his shoulder every turn he took.

It was all Captain Hefferson's fault, he thought. Hefferson and that damn war. If it wasn't for them, he'd have his own farm, with a feather bed to sleep on and a warm woman to share it. He told himself that when he got the money, this time he'd really do it. He'd really up and buy himself a farm and find himself a woman, instead of letting the loot slip through his fingers in some damn saloon. He wondered if Weenie would consider being a farmer's wife.

It didn't seem likely.

Now it seemed unlikely he'd ever catch up with the Bordeaux brothers. Unlikely he'd ever find the horses. Unlikely he'd ever get anywhere except a prison cell, or a quick grave.

Lifting his head, he looked at the sky. The sun glared at him. The morning, and his whole life, were slipping past. He'd sure as hell never stand a chance of getting anywhere if he just sat letting it happen. Hefting himself to his feet, he searched out the trail of the lost horses.

He'd walked a good mile before he spotted them. They were together, grazing contentedly in a low between two ridges. As he saw them, they spotted him. Tossing up their heads, they gazed at him. Then, as if at a signal, all three wheeled and ran.

Wearily, he followed.

The horses moved on, keeping a distance ahead of him, keeping within his sight, tantalizing him.

Finally he decided this was no good. This way, he'd end up walking them to California without ever laying a hand on them. He sat down to consider.

The horses went calmly to grazing again.

A man afoot was a pitiful creature, he thought. He remembered the sheriff and Stacy, and how he had taken off with their horses, leaving them in the middle of nowhere. He felt sorry for them. But, hell, they could shank it back to Jack Hollow and pick up where they'd left off. All he could do was go on. And on and on and on.

He studied the horses thoughtfully. There was no point in pushing them farther west. If he had to walk them, at least he could head them back toward camp. Rising, he set out to swing wide around them and come up on their far side.

They eyed him until he disappeared behind a patch of trees, then returned to their grazing.

It was a long walk. He was tired. Sick and tired of the whole damn business. Almost ready to give in and give up. Let the sheriff come find him and take him prisoner again. Only he couldn't even be sure of that. Maybe the sheriff had gone back to Jack Hollow and nobody was hunting him, and he and Weenie could wait until Doomsday without getting help.

He had to catch the horses, not just for himself, but for Weenie.

He moved on, coming up to the west of the horses. As they saw him, they edged away, back the way they'd come.

He kept after them, walking slowly, calling and coaxing. And cursing. Each time he stepped toward them, they drifted on away from him.

While the coffee boiled, Weenie combed her hair. She washed her face and applied light touches of paint to her cheeks and lips. Studying her reflection in the metal travel mirror she'd brought along, she was far from satisfied.

She wanted to be pretty for Collin. She'd gotten him into this mess. Now there was nothing she could do to help him. She felt useless and foolish, like a geegaw meant to sit on a mantelpiece and be ornate, but not good for anything else. She couldn't help him catch the horses. She couldn't even make a pot of coffee for him. All she could do in life was look pretty, act charming, and make love. Now, here, she wasn't even pretty. She looked like some hag of a prairie woman, all weather-beaten and sunburned, with her lips cracked and her skin getting rough and flaky, and her hair like a bird's nest.

She felt like crying.

A sudden sound grabbed her attention. The coffee was boiling over. She snatched at the pot. The handle was hot. Too hot. As she pulled the pot off the fire, it burned her fingers. Wincing, she jerked them away. The pot fell over, spilling the coffee into the fire.

It was ruined. All ruined. Sucking on her fingers, she bawled in despair.

After a while, she decided she couldn't let Collin come back and find everything like this. She'd have coffee ready for him, and breakfast, too. Somehow.

Recalling the way Collin had done it, she got the fire going again, and got coffee cooking over it. Then she

170

began rummaging through the supplies for something to make breakfast out of.

There was a sack of dried beans, another of flour, and a wrapped slab of fry. She didn't know what to do with any of them. Sadly, she set them aside as useless. It would have been nice to have a pan of fry and hot bread for Collin. She thought she really should learn to cook. She decided to do it the first chance she got.

She hoped she'd have a chance. But if Tuck Tobin caught up with her and captured her, she'd surely go to prison. She didn't think she could stand prison. She'd rather be dead. If she were caught, she'd kill herself.

That idea horrified her.

She wondered how Collin could stand living the way he did, with the threat of prison or death always riding his shoulder.

Poor Collin. Poor dear sweet Collin.

Sorting the airtights, she found one of sweetened peaches. At the sight of it, and the thought of the juicy fruit inside, she realized how terribly hungry she was.

She opened the can hurriedly, and picked out a piece of peach with her bare fingers. It was delicious. As she licked her fingers, she thought that Ida Red would never approve. A proper lady didn't do such things. She picked out another piece, not caring what a proper lady wouldn't do.

She could smell the coffee boiling. She looked proudly at the pot. She didn't feel like a *lady* now. She felt like a *woman*. Collin McKay's woman, fixing his food for him while he tended to a man's chores. She ate one more bit of peach and sipped a little syrup, meaning to keep the rest for Collin.

Suddenly she saw a horse.

It was ambling over the ridge. And there were the other two horses behind it.

"Collin!" she called eagerly.

He didn't answer.

The horses came on toward her, slowing their pace, eyeing her warily. But Collin didn't appear.

She thought something must have happened to him. He could be lying injured somewhere, needing help. She had to find him. Gathering her skirts, she started for the ridge.

She stopped short. If Collin were hurt, he might need a doctor. She'd have to get him to a town. She'd have to have a horse. Somehow she had to catch a horse.

The horses halted. They stood bunched, gazing at her curiously.

Holding the can of peaches out at arm's length, she called, "Nice horsey. Here, horsey, come have a peach."

Tuck Tobin's bay glanced back the way it had come. Stacy's horse, a blaze-faced bay, gave a snort. But Weenie's sorrel filly sniffed the air and took a dainty step toward her.

"Nice horsey," she coaxed.

The filly studied her a moment, then began moving slowly toward her. The others hesitated. They followed cautiously. The filly came up to Weenie. The others stopped and watched.

Thrusting out its muzzle, the filly nosed at the airtight. Weenie flinched. The can slipped out of her fingers. Peaches and sweet syrup spilled on the ground.

Pleased, the filly lipped up a piece of peach. The blaze-faced bay came up then. It gave the sorrel a shove, trying to get at the sweets.

Weenie had no idea what to do now. She didn't have a bridle, and even if she'd had one, she wasn't sure she'd be able to get it onto the horse. But she had to do something.

She lifted her top skirt. With both hands, she tugged at the hem of a petticoat. She grunted as it gave.

The sound of ripping cloth startled the horses. Tossing up their heads, they backstepped away from Weenie.

"Nice horsey!" she breathed as she tore a strip from the petticoat. "Nice horsey!"

The filly rolled its eyes at her. It flared its nostrils, scenting the peaches. Then it nosed at the ground, hunting another sweet bit.

Weenie touched its neck. It stood. Carefully, she slipped the strip of cloth around its neck. It had found a peach. It paid no attention to her. Fingers trembling, she knotted the cloth. Then, experimentally, she gave a tug. The filly raised its head and eyed her reproachfully.

Now what? She looked hopefully toward the ridge and called again. "Collin! Please, Collin! Where are you?"

To her relief, she heard his voice. "Weenie! What's wrong? What's happened?"

He came jogging over the ridge. At the sight of the horses, he pulled up short. Soft-voiced, he called, "Hold'em, Weenie! Don't let'em get away!"

She nodded. She was holding the sorrel.

Tuck Tobin's bay nosed at the heap of saddles. The blaze-faced bay nibbled up the last of the spilled peaches, then raised its head and looked back at Collin.

He was coming up quietly behind it. The bridles were over his shoulder. He held a rein end ready in his hand.

The blaze-faced bay hesitated as he neared. He held a cupped hand toward it. Curious, it reached out to nose at the hand.

With a twist of his wrist, Collin slung the rein end around its neck. It jerked back. At the pull of the leather, it realized it was caught. Nickering, it gave in.

Collin sighed. He looked at Weenie and grinned.

The sorrel filly tugged at the rag Weenie had around its neck. She held tight. The filly surrendered and rubbed its cheek against her arm. Frightened but determined, she stood firm.

Collin bridled the blaze-faced bay and traded Weenie the reins for the rag she held. He hurriedly got a bridle on the filly, then turned to look for Tuck Tobin's horse.

It had disappeared.

For an instant, that fact chilled him. He felt as if it were an omen. Tobin would get the horse back, and would recapture him.

He told himself that was foolishness. Aloud, he said, "To hell with it."

"With what?" Weenie asked.

174

"The other horse. It was just trouble anyway." He held the sorrel's reins out to her. "Here, you hold them while I get the saddles on them."

Instead of accepting the reins, she flung herself against him. Her arms wrapped around his neck. Her face pressed into his shoulder. She began to bawl.

"It's all right, Weenie," he told her. "It's all right now. We got the horses. We'll be all right."

"I — I — oh, Collin," she sobbed. "Collin, I'm sorry!"

"What for?" he asked gently. "What's wrong?"

"The horses! They ate your breakfast!"

CHAPTER
FOURTEEN

Tuck woke to the brightness of the full moon overhead. He lay in Stacy's arms and wished that this were all of life, all of the world. He'd be content to spend forever here, now, in this quiet moment.

But there was no way.

He had a job to do. He had to capture McKay and Weenie and return the bank loot to Jack Hollow. He had to prove himself to the town and to Curly Hobbs. He had to win an election.

Why?

Because there was nothing else in his life. Nothing except Stacy. And last night she'd refused him. She slept with him. Let him love her. But she wouldn't marry him.

He didn't want to think about that. He tried to concentrate on the job. If he woke her now, they could get on the trail again. Track by moonlight. Maybe catch up with McKay and Weenie. Follow close behind them and let them lead the way to the money. Be on hand to take it.

Then what?

The small ugly thought that had edged around his awareness forced itself before him. For the first time, he faced it. He was certain the fight between Weenie and Stacy had been staged to draw attention away from the bank robbery. Weenie had plotted it with the robbers.

What if Stacy had been in on the plot?

The thought hurt. If she had been a part of the robbery, then he had a duty to accuse her. He'd have to arrest her, see her brought to trial. He didn't think he could do it.

He tried telling himself she hadn't known, Weenie had tricked her into the fight. But last night she'd said things, and there were things she hadn't said, and it all implied too much. She wanted money. A lot of money. She didn't want Tuck Tobin. She didn't want him enough to accept him as he was, with nothing more than what he had to offer her. Yet she'd insisted on trailing along with him after McKay and Weenie. Why? Because he could help her trail McKay to the money?

Then what?

Too many questions. Painful questions. He didn't want to think. He didn't want to consider the possibilities.

He thought of turning back now, taking Stacy to Jack Hollow and forgetting the bank loot. But he'd be going in defeat, to Curly Hobbs's ridicule. And what of Stacy?

Questions without answers.

He stirred restlessly. Stacy's arms tightened around him. Still sleeping, she nuzzled at his neck. He pressed his face to hers, wishing there were some way to run from the questions. Escape them. Leave them behind, unanswered and forgotten.

At last he slept again.

When the dawn woke him, he felt weary with uncertainties. It bothered him that Stacy was bright and vital, eager to be on the trail again. That seemed somehow to confirm his suspicions of her. Sullenly, he saddled the horse and gave her a hand up. With a sense of futility, he walked ahead, hunting sign, going on with the search, wondering what its end would be.

The traces of sign led them to a peak of rock. Behind it they found horse gear heaped on the ground near the ashes of a campfire. The gear was Tuck's own. The war bag of supplies had been taken from the saddle, and the Winchester from its boot, but the rest was there. And around them were fresh hoofprints.

From the sign, Tuck read that two horses with riders had left together. The third horse had run loose in a different direction. He thought the loose horse was his own bay. He told Stacy to wait. Carrying the bridle, he set out to find the horse.

He found it about a mile from the campsite, grazing contentedly. He called as he approached, and it recognized him. It stood for him, accepting the bit.

Riding horseback, he returned to Stacy.

She was on the ground, studying the sign Collin and Weenie had left. When she saw Tuck, she shouted, "They're not very far ahead! Now we've both got horses, it'll be easy to catch up!"

He nodded and slid down off the bay's back. Scooping up his saddle, he swung it into place and bent to catch a cinch. When he looked up again, Stacy had already mounted the gray and sat waiting.

"You're in a hell of a hurry, aren't you?" he said.

"Aren't you?" she asked.

He jerked a latigo tight, then turned to face her. "When we get the money, what then?"

"What do you mean?"

Suddenly his anger was gone. All he felt was his caring for her. "Stacy, you've got a horse and supplies. It's not a far ride across the line to Morrison. You could go there. Go on from there somewhere else. Start over. Forget this whole business."

"What on earth are you talking about?"

"If you get your hands on that money, there's only one way you'll really be safe. You'll have to see us all dead. Don't you understand that? McKay and Weenie could always implicate you. I'm the law. I'd have a duty to go after you. You'd have to kill us all. Is that what you want?"

She gazed at him, her face unreadable. Finally she said, "You think I had a part in the robbery?"

"You did, didn't you?"

"Can you really believe that, Tuck?"

"It's not easy. No easier than believing you really love me."

"Oh, Tuck!" Swinging herself down off the gray, she flung herself into his arms. "Oh, God, Tuck!"

He held her, wanting to believe he was wrong. Almost believing.

Softly, he asked her, "Will you marry me?"

"Yes."

He told himself it was the truth. But a part of his mind insisted that she could be lying. There wasn't any way he could know for sure, not until it had been done.

Or he'd been betrayed. All he could do now was go on and see.

He kissed her gently. Hopefully.

Together, they rode on.

As Collin and Weenie rode westward, the land was changing. The ridges were no longer so sharp, the draws so deep. There was more grass and brush here, and occasional stands of trees gave moments of shade.

It was midafternoon when Collin halted in the pines and told Weenie, "It's just over the next rise."

"What is?"

"The hideout. The place I told you about."

"You told me it had a spring, didn't you? Good water?"

He nodded.

"Could we stop awhile? Long enough for me to take a bath? Please, Collin?"

He lifted a brow at her and smiled at the thought of sharing a bath in the spring with her. But he supposed he couldn't risk that. While she bathed, he'd have to stand guard.

He said, "Depends. If things look clear and there's no sign of that damn sheriff behind us, maybe we can take the time."

"I've got to have a bath. Collin, you know Tuck and Stacy are probably back in Jack Hollow now, all nice and comfortable with hot baths and good meals and soft beds, and they're not even thinking about us at all."

"Maybe," he allowed, hoping she was right. "You wait here. Hold the horses. I'll scout ahead. If it's clear, I'll come right back for you."

"You think somebody might be there?"

"Likely not," he said, sliding out of the saddle. He handed her his reins. "But I got no mind to take chances. You hang on to this horse. Whatever you do, don't let him get away from you."

She nodded and worked up a weary smile for him.

Past the edge of the pines, the land rose to a rolling ridge. Carrying the Winchester, Collin walked to it and looked out at the ruins of the old trading post.

There had been cleared land, pasturage, around the place once. Now it was a wide expanse of long grass, weeds, and young trees, skirted by stands of pine. The remains of the building stood in the middle of the clearing.

The trading post had been a single large L-shaped building. Winter snows had collapsed parts of the roof, but the heavy log walls were still solid. The small square window openings were once fitted with shutters. The leather hinges had rotted. The shutters lay on the ground, overgrown with weeds. The water hole was a fair-sized pond fed by a natural spring. It lay in the angle of the L, its banks lush green. Game trails were worn through the grass to it.

From the ridge, Collin surveyed the place warily. It looked every bit as abandoned as it ever had. Even so, he was cautious as he worked his way to the ruins.

Reaching a wall, he leaned against it and listened. The faint sounds from inside could have been made by rats and bats and other small creatures that made the place home. Or by someone hiding inside.

Collin didn't think the sheriff could have outguessed him and got here ahead of him. But there were other men like Collin who knew the place as a hideout far from the traveled trails. Secretive men who might be friends today and enemies tomorrow. Men who might not welcome company of any stripe.

Rifle cocked, he sidled to a window and looked in.

He found himself face to face with a horse.

Startled, he jerked back. His heart gave a jump that pulled a cramp through his chest. He pressed his shoulder blades against the wall. Swallowing hard, he sucked in a deep breath to ease the cramp. He was getting awful jumpy these days, he told himself. Too damn jumpy for this kind of business.

The horse thrust its head through the window and gazed curiously at him. It was a filly, the head small and well shaped, with a bald face and one moon eye. Traces of dried sweat showed where a bridle had been not long ago.

Nothing else happened. Collin and the horse stared at each other. After a moment, Collin gently nudged the horse's head out of the way and peered past it into the building.

Sunlight filtered through the broken roof into what had been the common room of the trading post. Debris of the roof cluttered much of the dirt floor. In a clear corner, where the roof was still whole, lay a crumpled blanket and a saddle. Collin frowned at them. It was a sidesaddle.

Shoving the horse back, he scanned as much of the room as he could see. There was no sign of the woman who'd ridden that saddle. He thought she must be around somewhere. He edged toward the next window.

"Collin McKay!" she exclaimed.

He wheeled, and there she was, behind him.

Minnie Evans.

She was a small, fine-boned blonde of much the same style as Weenie Greenwood, with pale blue eyes and full pouty pink lips.

She was wearing a riding habit that matched the color of her eyes. In one hand she carried a closed parasol trimmed with fluffy ruffles. In the other she held a nickel-plated Remington revolver. It was the new line model that held five .30 rimfire shorts. Sunlight glittered on its barrel. It was aimed at Collin's chest. He could see the noses of the loads in the cylinders.

"Put that down, Collin," she said sweetly, dipping the little pistol just enough to indicate the Winchester he held. Then she leveled it at his chest again.

He didn't doubt that she was capable of putting those five pieces of lead into him with a steady hand.

Gently, he eased the Winchester off cock and leaned it against the wall. Hands empty, he lifted his gaze from the pistol to Minnie's face. He thought he saw indecision flickering behind her eyes.

What the hell was she up to, he wondered.

"Minnie," he said cautiously. "It ain't nice to point a gun at a man that way."

She made her decision. Suddenly she flung herself against him, wrapping her arms around his neck.

"Oh, Collin! I'm so glad to see you. They're after me. You've got to help me."

"Who's after you?" he asked. Her body was soft and pleasant against his. But the gun in her hand was a hard lump pressing into his back. He thought that even at that angle she could do him a lot of damage if she pulled the trigger.

"Lyle and Bull. Collin, you've got to help me. They'll kill me!" She squirmed against him.

He kissed her. It was a deep, fierce kiss that held her mouth for a long moment. When he finally drew back, she eased her grip on him. She looked up into his face with a confident smile.

The gun was no longer digging into his back. Now it rested loosely in the hand she had on his shoulder.

He ducked suddenly, twisting, grabbing her arm. His hand locked over her wrist and wrenched. The gun slipped out of her grip. As it thudded on the ground, he bent to scoop it up.

She hit him on the head with her parasol.

Grunting, he grabbed the little pistol and leveled it at her.

She had the parasol raised to strike again. She stood there, holding it over her head, her mouth agape, her eyes wide.

Her expression shifted from fury to appalled innocence. "Collin, whatever —"

"It ain't nice to point a gun at a man," he said. "It ain't nice to hit him on the head, neither. Minnie, where's the money?"

184

For an instant the anger flashed in her face again. Recovering her baby-doll innocence, she said, "What money?"

He hefted the revolver and looked at it. A pretty little thing. Small for his hand. Big for hers.

"The money you took off the Bordeaux brothers."

"I don't know what you're talking about."

"Sure you do. If the Bordeaux boys still had it, you'd be with them, making up to Lyle for a piece of it. If they're chasing you now, meaning you harm, it's because you've got the money away from them."

She sniffed, and two small tears appeared on her lashes. Collin found himself resenting that. It was as if she were mocking Weenie.

"You got the money with you, ain't you?" he said.

"I don't know what you're talking about," she insisted.

"Minnie, Bull tried to kill me. He ran out on me and took my share of that bank loot. He left me for the law. I didn't take none to kindly to that."

"Then you'll help me?"

"I mean to have my share of that money."

"I wouldn't keep it from you, Collin." Dropping the parasol, she held both arms toward him. "I wouldn't keep anything from you."

A sudden shout cut the air. *"Collin McKay!"*

Collin winced. He saw Weenie astride her own mount, hauling his horse along at the ends of its reins. She was racing toward the trading post, bouncing in the saddle, skirts flapping, eyes blazing.

185

Minnie's arms were around Collin's neck. She clung tight. With a muttered curse, he shoved her away.

Jerking her horse up short, Weenie glared at Collin. "Of all the double-dealing, two-timing, low-living, useless, worthless sons of she-hound, you — you — !"

As she reined up, the horse she was leading ran past her. It almost overran Collin. He jumped aside and grabbed it by the bridle.

Brought up short, the horse swung its rump around. It rammed into Minnie. She let out a squeal as she stumbled, almost falling.

"Whoa, boy, easy there," Collin crooned at the horse.

Minnie steadied herself. She picked up her parasol, opened it, and set it jauntily over her shoulder. From its shade, she looked up at Weenie. "Well now, what have we here?"

"Trouble," Collin mumbled to himself as he glanced from one woman to the other. It occurred to him that a man could be a damn sight worse off with two women than with none at all.

"Minnie Evans, isn't it?" Weenie said. She nodded toward the ruins. "Is this where you're working now, Minnie dear? How wonderful! You've really come up in the world."

"My, what an original hairdo, dearie," Minnie said. "Your own creation?"

"This certainly is an improvement over the last cow crib you were thrown out of, isn't it, Minnie dear?"

"What *is* that scent you're wearing? Horse piss?"

"*Money!*" Collin interrupted.

Both women looked at him in puzzlement.

186

"Money," he repeated. "That's what we're all here about, ain't it?"

The women glanced warily at each other. Neither answered.

"Hell, with that sheriff likely coming after us from one direction," Collin said, looking at Weenie. He turned to Minnie. "And the Bordeaux boys coming from the other, we ain't got a lot of time to stand around here jawing. Minnie, you got the money on your saddle?"

Reluctantly, she said, "I hid it."

He cocked a brow at her. The way he figured, once she got her hands on all that cash, she'd never let go. There'd been gold and banknotes both, too much bulk and weight for her to have it hidden in her skirts. So it had to be in her traveling gear.

Amiably, he said, "All right. I'll get your horse saddled up, and we'll go somewhere else to augur over it."

Turning, he stalked toward the door of the common room.

"I'll do it, Collin," Minnie said, hurrying after him. "I can take care of my own horse."

As Collin walked into the common room, the filly stepped toward him. It limped.

"Like hell you can," he grumbled at Minnie. "So that's why you holed up here. You lamed your horse."

"Collin, help me, please!" Minnie grabbed his arm. "I've got to get away from here. You have horses. We can go together."

"I have horses?"

"Uh huh. I could ride the horse that — that *woman* is on."

"You want to leave Weenie stranded here?"

Minnie slithered her hand up his arm. She slid it across his chest and in between the buttons of his shirt.

"Just you and me, Collin darling. And the money."

It had been Lyle and her until the money came along. Collin thought suddenly that he'd rather have Weenie without the money than Minnie with it. But he had hopes of Weenie and the money both.

"We got to get out of here quick, before trouble shows up," he said, pulling away from Minnie.

He bent and lifted the filly's lame hoof. "You got a knife or something like one?"

"What?"

"There's nothing wrong with your horse, only she's got a pebble caught under her shoe. I need something to pry it out with. She'll have a bruise, but likely she'll be able to travel."

"I'll get something."

Minnie fumbled through her gear. She brought out a pearl-handled penknife. It was a tiny thing. Collin pinched out the blade. Hoping it wouldn't snap in his fingers, he dug at the pebble with it.

"You get your stuff together," he told Minnie.

She busied herself rolling the crumpled blanket and stowing odds and ends in a war bag. She had made a messy camp. She built a messy bedroll.

Collin had the filly saddled and bridled, ready and waiting, by the time Minnie finished her packing. Along with the war bag, she had two sets of saddlebags. One was the small kind made for a sidesaddle, fitting over the pommel, with a single pocket on the horse's off side. The other was cut on the line of Army issue, but bigger. It was the kind Bull Bordeaux had put the bank money in. The same one, Collin thought. Minnie handed him the little one.

While he fastened it to the pommel, he watched her heft the big one over the horse's rump. She snugged it to the cantle and lashed it in place securely. Pretending he was still occupied with attaching the pommel bag, Collin let her put on the war bag and bedroll herself. She didn't seem so particular about them.

Weenie was waiting outside. She had gotten herself off her horse and stood wearily against the wall, holding the reins, letting both mounts nibble at the lush weeds.

At the sight of Minnie's sidesaddle, she stiffened. Her eyes narrowed and her mouth quivered. She glared at Collin as if he'd done her some harm.

"Come on," he said. "Let's get moving."

Minnie looked expectantly at him.

He realized she was waiting for a hand up. Hell, she'd got this far on her own. But there was no time for auguring. He laced his fingers and gave her the cup of his hands as a step.

She let out a startled squeak at the roughness with which he boosted her up to the saddle.

He turned to Weenie to offer her the step of his hands.

"Don't you touch me," she said. She grabbed her saddle horn and bounced on one foot, hunting the stirrup with the other.

She'd never mounted from the ground without help before. She had difficulty enough getting off her horse unaided. Her face reddened as she bounced without success.

She'd never make it, Collin thought. He started to force his help on her.

Somehow she got a toe into the stirrup. As Collin reached for her, she hefted up. For a moment she was lying on her belly across the saddle, flailing the other leg in an effort to get it over the horse's rump.

Collin stifled a laugh.

Minnie heehawed, loud and nasty.

Getting her leg where it belonged, Weenie straightened herself in the saddle. Her face was very red. Head high, she lifted rein and gigged her horse.

"Where are you going?" Collin called at her.

She didn't know. She pulled rein. But she refused to look back at Collin.

Collecting the Winchester, he swung up onto his own horse and turned it toward the nearest point of trees. "This way."

Minnie moved her horse up close behind him.

Weenie looked around. She frowned as she squinted into the distance. Rising in her stirrups, she pointed and called, "Collin, look!"

He looked over his shoulder.

Two riders had appeared on a ridge. The Bordeaux brothers.

CHAPTER
FIFTEEN

"Run!" Collin shouted at the women.

The Bordeaux brothers had spotted them and were racing downslope toward them.

Clinging to her saddle with one hand, Weenie used the other to lash at her mount's flanks with the rein ends. The horse bolted for the woods. She didn't try to control it, only to stay on and keep it running.

Without hesitation, Minnie started after her. But the filly's stone-bruised hoof was sore. As she drove it into a gallop, the horse lurched lopsidedly and tossed its head in protest.

Collin held tight rein on his horse and faced toward the Bordeaux brothers. His heart hammered hard in his chest. He wanted to run. But he had to protect the women, give them a chance to get clear.

He jerked up the Winchester and snapped off a shot, hoping it would scare the Bordeaux boys, slow them down some.

It didn't. They plunged headlong toward him.

He flung another wild shot at them, then spurred his horse toward the woods. He meant to make it to cover and make a stand. He had the rifle that was in his hands and a carbine in his saddle boot. If the Bordeaux boys tried to follow, he'd be able to pick them off.

Even as he thought it, he realized he didn't want to do it. He had never killed a man. He didn't want to do it now. Not even a Bordeaux. He'd sooner run. Escape. Get away with the money and forget the Bordeaux boys.

He just didn't have the grit for it, he thought sadly.

Behind him, he heard the blast of a rifle.

Something slammed into his back, throwing him off balance. Suddenly he was numb. Tumbling out of the saddle. Falling. Sprawling on the ground.

Hazily, he saw his horse racing on, stirrups flapping. He saw Minnie Evans at the edge of the woods. She looked back. At him. At the Bordeaux brothers. Drawing rein, she turned back.

Collin tried to struggle up. He made it onto one elbow as Minnie rode past him.

"Minnie!" he breathed hoarsely. "Help me!"

If she heard him, she paid him no mind. Over his shoulder, he watched her hurry on toward the Bordeaux brothers.

"Lyle!" She screeched. "Oh, Lyle, thank God you've found me! I've been so frightened! They *kidnapped* me!"

A man damn well couldn't trust anybody, Collin thought darkly. Not even himself. He felt ashamed of having called for her help.

The numbness he felt was yielding to pain. A small spot of pain started in his back at his left shoulder blade. It spread out until his whole back ached. He wondered how badly he'd been wounded. He didn't suppose it mattered. He couldn't get away now. He was as good as dead. He hoped the Bordeaux brothers would get it over with quick, finish him off where he lay. He hoped he could take it, not break and beg.

It was all Captain Hefferson's fault, he told himself. Hefferson and that damn war. Sighing, he let his head sink down onto his outstretched arm. He closed his eyes and waited.

He heard Minnie and the Bordeaux brothers come together. He heard her gasping breathlessly as she told them a long windy about Collin and Weenie forcing her at gunpoint, stealing the money and dragging her along and scaring hell out of her, and how glad she was to be in Lyle's arms again.

It sounded like Lyle believed every word, but Bull was a mite doubtful. Collin thought it was damn bitchy of Minnie to mention Weenie that way after Weenie had managed to escape into the woods, maybe get completely clear.

Then he heard Bull saying something about catching Weenie.

Collin didn't want that to happen. He couldn't let it happen. There had to be some way he could slow the Bordeaux boys down. Take their minds off Weenie.

He'd had the Winchester in his hand when he came off his horse. He thought he must have dropped it close by. Forcing open his eyes, he saw long grass. It was in front of his face, blocking his vision. Cautiously, he tried lifting his head. The pain in his back spread its

193

claws, digging at him like a bobcat. Biting his lip, he gazed at the ground directly in front of him.

The rifle wasn't there. With effort, he craned his neck to look around.

He spotted the gun in the grass not far from his foot. He couldn't help a grunt of pain as he began to squirm slowly around. He hoped he'd be able to reach it.

As he moved, he was aware that both arms worked. His legs seemed to work, too. He thought maybe he wasn't shot up as bad as he felt. He wondered if he had a chance to pull through this mess after all. Maybe he could get the gun. Shoot the Bordeaux boys. Something. Maybe.

He managed to turn. He was almost in a position to reach for the rifle when he saw boots. The toes pointed toward him. One of the Bordeaux boys was standing there, looking down at him.

Propped on his elbows, Collin frowned at the boots. Sighing, he slumped a bit. Then, suddenly, with a thrust of his elbows against the ground, he lunged at them. As he fell toward them, he rolled enough to lash out with his right arm.

A sharp rowel ripped at his wrist as he hooked the arm around the boots just above the spurs. Still rolling, he dragged with all his strength.

Bull Bordeaux let out a ridiculously high-pitched squeal as his legs were jerked from under him.

He landed on his rump with a sharp grunted curse.

Collin was on his side now. He saw Bull hit ground. He saw the expression on Bull's face. It was as foolish as the squeal. Collin began to laugh.

Laughing hurt. But he couldn't help it. He pressed his face into the crook of his arm, gasping and laughing.

Somebody kicked him. Lyle, he thought. The kick was a small discomfort compared to the bobcat pain clawing at his back. A ridiculous kick. Somehow everything seemed ridiculous.

He heard a jangle of spur chains as Bull got himself onto his feet. Then he heard Bull growl, "What the hell is so goddamned funny?"

Collin managed to collect enough breath to answer, "You."

Sounding bewildered, Lyle said, "He's crazy."

"You're crazy, McKay," Bull rasped. "You're shot, maybe dying, and you're laughing. You're crazy."

Collin felt lightheaded, drunkenly giddy. The pain in his back was growing oddly distant. He didn't think the wound was serious. Nothing seemed serious. With his face still pressed against his arm, and his ribs still heaving, he mumbled, "I ain't dying."

"If you ain't now, you damned well will be when I'm done with you," Bull told him. "Get up."

Collin wondered if he could get up. He wasn't sure. Curious, he decided to give it a try.

Lifting his head, he braced himself on his elbows. He drew up one leg, then the other. Slowly, pressing his hands to the ground, he got himself onto his knees. His success so far pleased him. He looked proudly up at Bull Bordeaux.

Bull was standing in front of him. Lyle was a bit to one side. Minnie clung to Lyle's arm. Bull's face was dark with embarrassed rage. Lyle looked puzzled. Minnie looked scared as hell.

Collin began to laugh again.

"It ain't funny!" Bull insisted. There was fury in his voice. The icy fury of a vain man who'd been made a fool. And there was desperation at his helplessness, his inability to stop Collin's laughter.

Minnie suggested, "Kill him."

Collin looked at her. "You afraid I'll tell them the truth, Minnie?"

"What truth?" Lyle asked.

"Ask her," Collin said. And he laughed.

Minnie turned wide eyes up to Lyle. Her expression was as innocent as she could make it. "I've told you the truth. He'll tell you a lot of lies to try to save his own skin."

Lyle nodded in agreement with her.

"Look here, McKay," Bull growled. His revolver was in his hand, the muzzle aimed at Collin's head.

Collin had been looking at Lyle and Minnie. He saw the gun from the corner of his eye. He heard the scear catch as the hammer was drawn back to full cock.

Suddenly he didn't feel like laughing any more. Not at all. Suddenly he felt like begging. Pleading. Crawling with his face in the dirt, if that was what Bull wanted.

And then he felt disgust with himself. He knew Bull wanted him to crawl. But he wouldn't give Bull that satisfaction. No, dammit, he wouldn't back down and die crawling. Bull would sure as hell kill him, no matter what. At least he could die decent, like a man.

He caught his breath. Forcing himself, he laughed again. Laughed at Bull.

"Look here at this!" Bull repeated, shaking the gun.

Collin refused to look directly at it.

The scear clicked again as Bull eased down the gun hammer. For a moment, Collin was puzzled. Then he saw Bull lift the gun. Bull held it up long enough to be sure Collin understood his intention. Long enough for Collin to anticipate the blow.

In that instant, Collin understood just how deeply he'd injured Bull's vanity with his laughter. He knew Bull would never let him die easy now.

The gun slammed down against Collin's head, smashing him into darkness.

Very slowly, Collin became aware of the smell of coffee cooking. It was morning, he thought, and somebody was making breakfast, and everything else had been a dream. He'd had some kind of nightmare about the Bordeaux brothers shooting him in the back. He could still feel the pain. He thought that once he managed to wake up, the pain would go away.

He understood that he was lying on his back. It felt like he was on top of something sharp. He wanted to roll over and get off it. But he couldn't.

He came completely awake with the realization that he was tied, lashed spread-eagle on the ground.

He wasn't alone. He heard Bull Bordeaux say something. He couldn't make out the words. Then Bull chuckled.

"Would you really do that to him?" That was Lyle's voice.

"Hell," Bull grunted. "Why not?"

"It's awful rough," Lyle answered.

"I'm a rough man," Bull said proudly.

There was a moment of silence. Then Lyle called, "Hey, Minnie, ain't that coffee ready yet?"

"Just about," she replied.

Collin wondered if maybe they'd give him some. He doubted it. He sure as hell could use a drink of coffee. He felt dazed. Lying with his eyes closed, he tried to assemble the misty thoughts and broken recollections that scudded through his mind.

It was no nightmare. It was real. He had been shot in the back. He was their prisoner now. Before long, he'd be dead.

And that was that.

He heard the sound of coffee being poured. He heard one of the men grunt, then sigh with satisfaction. God, he wanted a taste of that coffee. He didn't think they'd kill him outright. He wondered whether they'd leave him tied up to starve, or think of something worse.

There were the sounds of boots on the earth and the jangle of spur chains. Coming toward him. He sensed the presence of someone towering over him. He smelled stale sweat and hot coffee.

Suddenly something seared his face. With a yelp, he jerked his head aside.

"He's awake now," Bull Bordeaux said.

Collin twisted his neck, rubbing his cheek against his outstretched arm, trying to wipe away the sting of the hot coffee that had been poured into his face. He'd wanted some. But not that way. His eyes burned. Clenched shut, they washed themselves with tears. After a moment, he was able to squeeze them open.

Above him he saw a blur that he knew was Bull. He blinked, clearing his vision enough for him to see Bull's grin. A damn nasty grin. He thought it would be satisfying to laugh in Bull's face again. But he couldn't quite manage it.

"Bull," Minnie said. "Why don't you leave him alone?"

"Why don't you mind your own damned business?" Bull snapped back at her.

Collin hoped she'd argue in his behalf. She didn't even bother to reply.

Bull hadn't dumped the whole cup of coffee into Collin's face. He lifted the cup and sipped at what was left.

Collin glanced around. They were inside the common room of the old trading post. He was lying in the rubble under a large hole in the roof. His wrists were lashed between upright roof supports. His ankles were tied to a fallen beam, a huge, heavy rough-hewn timber.

Away from him, where the roof was still sound and the earthen floor under it clear, a small fire was burning. A string of smoke rose from it to curl under the roof and leak through the hole in almost invisible trickles. It wasn't likely anyone would notice the smoke and come investigate. Beyond the hole, the sky was dim, fading into twilight.

Collin guessed that the Bordeaux brothers would camp the night in the ruins. Likely they wouldn't kill him until morning. Not with Bull so damn vicious mad at him for that laughter. Bull would want to let him lie there and think about dying for a while before it happened. He had a feeling that by morning Bull might have him downright eager to be dead.

He shouldn't have laughed, he thought. But, dammit, at least he'd got back at Bull. If he could just hold out and die decent without whining, Bull would never forget that laughter. Bull would never forget Collin McKay.

Collin wished to hell he could work up one more good laugh at Bull before he died.

Cup in hand, Bull hunkered at Collin's side. The aroma of the coffee was strong. Collin glanced longingly at the cup.

With his free hand, Bull picked up something from the ground near Collin's side. He held it up where Collin could see it easily. It was a splintered bit of wood, a rotten piece of broken shingle from the roof.

"Kindling," Bull said. He put the stick down on Collin's belly. Then he began to pile more pieces on top of Collin, and between his spread legs.

CHAPTER
SIXTEEN

Weenie whipped frantically at her horse with the rein ends, plunging it through the woods. She burst suddenly into a glade. As she raced across it, she realized no one was behind her.

Reaching the trees on the far side of the glade, she pulled the horse to a halt. She looked back over her shoulder. Collin wasn't hurrying after her. Neither was Minnie Evans. She couldn't see or hear any sign of anyone. She was alone.

The thought flashed through her mind that Collin had abandoned her. He had run off with that Minnie Evans and the money, and left her alone and helpless out here in the middle of nowhere.

Or —

She had heard shots. Collin could have been hit. He might be wounded. Even dead.

Suddenly she was certain he must have been shot. He wasn't the kind who'd run off and abandon her. He was dear and sweet, and no matter what Stacy said about men, Collin could be trusted. He had to have been shot, or he'd be here with her now. If he was hurt, he might need help.

She reined the horse around and rode slowly back to the other side of the glade. There, she struggled herself awkwardly out of the saddle. She tied her rein ends securely to a low tree limb. Gathering her skirts in both hands, she started through the woods. She walked softly, as silently as she could, back the way she had come.

She stopped short when she heard the grumble of voices. The two men speaking were the Bordeaux brothers. And Weenie couldn't mistake that simpering whine of Minnie Evans. She didn't hear Collin's voice.

Hurriedly, she hiked her skirts around her waist, twisting them into a bulky mass to hold them there. Heedless of the dirt and rubble under the trees, she dropped to the ground. On her hands and knees, she crept through the underbrush as cautiously as if she were sneaking up for a peek through a keyhole.

She saw them. It was only a glimpse, but it was enough. Minnie Evans was fawning over Lyle Bordeaux while Bull dragged the limp body of Collin McKay into the old trading post. There was blood on the back of Collin's shirt.

Weenie was on her knees. She rocked back onto her heels. Her vision blurred. She rubbed her knuckles at her eyes. It didn't do any good. The tears came, and kept coming.

Huddling in the brush, she pressed her face into her hands and cried.

Slowly a thought forced itself on her. It persisted until she faced it. Collin might be dead, but she wasn't.

She couldn't just linger here alone. She had to take care of herself. Go somewhere.

Still sobbing, she got to her feet and headed for her horse. She wasn't thinking about the problem of mounting it at all. She untied the reins and grabbed the saddle horn. Somehow, on the first try, she found herself in the saddle. Laying rein to the horse's neck, she turned it toward the east.

She knew one thing for certain. She had to stay away from the Bordeaux brothers. She rode slowly, quietly, picking her way through the woods. She kept going directly away from the old trading post until she was positive she would be well out of sight of it. Then she turned again, setting out in the direction she hoped would take her to the backtrail she and Collin had left. The direction she thought would eventually take her back to Jack Hollow.

She was still snuffling, still thinking of those horrible smears of blood on poor Collin's back, when she spotted the riders. There were two of them on a ridge, riding down it, disappearing into a hollow.

Halting, she rose in her stirrups and stared at the place where they'd disappeared. They'd only been blurs to her nearsighted eyes, but they were people. Living, breathing people. And she didn't think they were the Bordeaux brothers. Not coming from that direction.

She had to catch up with them.

Automatically, she patted at the tangled mat of her hair. She gave her rumpled skirts a jerk to neaten them, then slapped her horse into a lope.

The riders reappeared on a ridge. They were closer now. Easing her pace, Weenie waved and shouted at them.

They saw her and started toward her. As they came closer, she could see that one was riding a gray. She remembered the gray horse Collin had ridden out of Jack Hollow. Poor Collin. She'd never forgive herself for what had happened.

It occurred to her that this was the same horse. And she realized who was riding it. Stacy Kogh.

The man on the bay at Stacy's side was Tuck Tobin.

For an instant, Weenie's breath lumped in her throat. She'd stolen Tuck's prisoner and his horse and gun, and she'd run out on Stacy. She was in trouble. Bad trouble.

But she'd be in far worse trouble out here alone, or back in the hands of the Bordeaux brothers and Minnie Evans.

She rode on to meet Stacy and Tuck. By the time she reached them, she was crying bitterly. The tears were real.

As they came together, Tuck slid off his horse. He went to Weenie's side and offered her his hands. She came out of the saddle into his arms, pressing her face into his shoulder. It was good to be in a man's arms again. Comforting. But they weren't Collin's arms.

She sobbed as she thought that poor dear Collin would never hold her again.

"Whoa there, girl," Tuck murmured, flustered. He patted uncertainly at her back and looked up to Stacy for help.

Stacy sat her mount stiffly. She cocked a brow at Weenie, very suspicious of the tears. With a sharp edge to her voice, she said, "Weenie, where's Collin?"

"Dead!" Weenie gasped.

"What?" Stacy swung down from her horse and stepped to Weenie's side. Grabbing Weenie's arm, she pulled her away from Tuck.

Weenie blinked tearfully. "He's dead. They killed him."

"Who did?" Tuck asked.

"The Bordeaux brothers. The ones who robbed the bank with him." Even as she said it, Weenie knew it was a mistake. Now Tuck would know for certain that she'd had a part in the robbery. But it was too late to take the words back.

"Weenie," Tuck said. "You'd better tell me everything."

Weenie nodded. There was no use fighting it. She had gambled and she'd lost. She'd lost Collin and the money and everything. Now she'd go to jail. But there was no good to be had from betraying Stacy. She told her story slowly, hesitantly, crying when she needed a moment to think. She managed to tell enough to satisfy Tuck without admitting Stacy's part in it.

When she'd done, Stacy's eyes on her were appreciative. Gently, Stacy said, "Don't worry, Weenie. We'll take care of you. We'll take care of everything."

"Collin's dead," Weenie snuffled. No one could do anything about that.

Tuck was gazing off into the distance. He said, "Weenie, where are the guns?"

"What guns?"

"My Winchester. Stacy's carbine."

"Collin had them. I guess the Bordeaux brothers have them now."

He frowned at her. "Both of them?"

She nodded.

"What are you going to do?" Stacy asked him.

"They haven't got any idea we're out here. They don't know anyone's after them. Likely they'll camp the night in that old ruin. Stacy, you and Weenie stay here while I go ahead and look things over."

"I'm coming with you," Stacy said.

He looked at her. "They're armed and we're not, remember? It could be dangerous."

"I know. I won't let you go alone, Tuck," she said as she stepped onto her horse. "If you try to go on ahead without me, I'll follow you. I won't let you go alone."

He knew she meant it. Was it because she loved him, or was it because of the money? He gazed at her, trying to read an answer in her face. But even a face could lie. He knew he wouldn't really have his answer until he'd gotten the money.

Without speaking, he mounted up.

"Don't leave me here!" Weenie shrieked. She grabbed the reins of her horse and scrambled awkwardly into the saddle.

They followed Weenie's trail, riding back the way she'd come. It was twilight when they reached the woods, almost night dark within the cover of the trees. Dismounting, they led the horses.

206

Tuck halted when he caught scent of a fire. He told Stacy, "You and Weenie wait here with the horses while I take a look up ahead."

"I'm going with you —" she started.

"No," he interrupted. "You want to get me killed?"

"Of course not!"

"Then you listen. One man sneaking around is bound to make some noise. Two people would likely make twice as much noise. You understand?"

"Uh huh," she admitted reluctantly.

"Stacy, stay with me, please," Weenie said in a small, frightened voice.

Tuck said, "You understand from here on you've got to do what I tell you — exactly what I tell you — or else you might get us all killed?"

"Uh huh," Stacy repeated.

"You promise?"

"I promise."

"All right. You stay here. Don't move. If I'm not back in a couple of hours, or if you hear shooting, get. Go back to Jack Hollow. Understand?"

"Uh huh. Tuck, be careful."

"Don't worry. I will."

Moving cautiously, he worked his way through the trees toward the source of the smoke scent. It was full night when he reached the edge of the woods. The moon wasn't up yet, but there was starlight enough for him to see by.

He looked across a field of weeds and rubble at a long wall of the ruined trading post. A faint glow from within showed him the square hole of a window. The smell of coffee mingled with the smoke odor of the campfire.

He crept along the edge of the forest until he could see around the end of the wall. The building was in the shape of an L. He could make out four horses picketed in its angle. He figured one was the mount McKay had ridden. One would be Minnie Evans's horse. The others would belong to the Bordeaux brothers. Likely there was no one else around.

As Tuck watched, a man emerged from the building. He was carrying something that looked like a carbine. Leaning it against the wall, he began to unbutton his britches.

For a moment, Tuck thought of dashing out of the woods, grabbing the gun, and running like hell. But it was a damn-fool idea. He stood gazing longingly at the carbine.

When the man had buttoned up again, he picked up the gun and walked a slow circle around the ruins. Back in the angle of the L, he sat down with his back against the wall and the carbine across his knees. From his attitude, he looked like he didn't feel there was any need for a guard, but he was taking watch anyway.

Well, that accounted for one Bordeaux brother.

Tuck worked his way back to the far side of the building. He studied the land as best he could in the faint light before he dropped to his belly and began to crawl toward the ruins.

Suddenly he was thinking of Curly Hobbs. He wondered if Curly would have the guts to try something like this. Not likely, he told himself. With a sense of personal satisfaction, he reached the wall. Rising, he flattened himself against it.

Voices murmured within the building. Edging toward the window, Tuck chanced a look in.

The campfire burning inside the room was very small. It barely gave enough light for him to see the two people seated near it, a man with a woman nestled against him.

There was gear on the floor close to the fire: saddles, bedrolls, war bags, and a rifle. He thought the rifle was his own Winchester. He flexed his fingers, wanting the feel of a gun in them.

The man whispered to the woman. She nodded. Rising, she collected a bedroll. As she started to spread a soogan, she turned toward the window.

Tuck jerked back.

Standing pressed against the wall, he heard more murmurs. The woman giggled. There were small noises. Then the woman moaned softly.

Those two would be busy for a while, Tuck thought. In time, they'd be asleep. He wondered if, once they slept, he might be able to sneak in and lay hands on that rifle.

A horse nickered. Something moved in the angle of the L. Spur chains jangled.

Tuck realized that the guard had decided to take a stroll around the building. With the thought, he felt his heart knot in his chest. There he was, in the open, and unarmed.

As good as dead.

He hoped Stacy would obey orders. Go back to Jack Hollow. Stay alive.

But the jangling footsteps were fading off in the other direction, and Tuck understood that the guard was making his circuit of the building the long way around.

Crouching low, Tuck dashed across the open and lunged into the woods.

He made noise.

The guard came racing around the corner. Gun at ready, he scanned the weedy field. Looked toward the woods. Stared into darkness.

He let the gun in his hands dip. Satisfied he'd heard only a wild night creature, he continued on his round.

Tuck stood clinging to a tree, pressed tight against it. He waited motionless until the pounding of his heart had eased. Then he headed back to the place where he'd left the women with the horses.

From his hiding place, Pike watched Tuck dash for the woods. He gave a sad shake of his head. These young bucks nowadays blundered around like blind bears. In *his* day, a man who couldn't outsneak a Lakota didn't keep his hair on his head long enough for it to go gray.

He watched Bull Bordeaux run around the corner and stand like a damn-fool post, and he thought if he'd wanted he could have picked the man off then and there. At least the sheriff had the good luck to be up against an enemy no smarter than himself. Pike wondered who'd survive this night.

Once Bordeaux had returned to his place in the angle of the L, Pike moved. Slithering like a shadow from his hiding place, moving with the patience of a stalking cat, he began to work his way toward the building.

CHAPTER
SEVENTEEN

The hell of it, Collin thought, was that even with his back aching and all his misery and being scared sick of what Bull Bordeaux was planning for him come morning, he wanted a woman.

Minnie and Lyle were in the same room with him, across the banked campfire from where he was tied. He resented that. He figured they could at least have had the damn decency to go off into a different room. They were making too much noise. He wished they'd get it over with.

Angrily, he jerked at one bound hand. That was no good at all. It made his back hurt worse. But the pain wasn't nearly as bad as the fear.

He had a godawful urge to scream. But he sure as hell wasn't going to give Bull that satisfaction. Whatever they did to him, he'd take it. He'd die like a man.

Goddammit, he couldn't! He'd never be able to hold still and calmly burn, and he knew it. He had to get himself out of this mess somehow.

But there wasn't any way out. There just plain wasn't. And he'd die screaming.

He thought of Weenie. At least he'd managed to take Bull's mind off her. He hoped she'd got away safe. He hoped she'd remember him occasionally. Maybe be sad for him.

At last Minnie and Lyle were quiet. Soon one began to draw the slow steady breaths of deep sleep. Then the other began to snore.

Collin wished he could find sleep and escape all the thoughts and feelings that seethed in his mind. He closed his eyes but they didn't want to stay closed. After a while, he let them open and lay gazing at the sky beyond the hole in the roof. It was thick with stars. When he was a tad, his maw had told him each star was a guardian angel watching over someone on earth. He thought that if there was one for him, it sure didn't seem to be looking now.

This was going to be one hell of a long night.

He winced at a sudden small noise near his head. A rat, he thought. That was all he needed now. A damn rat to gnaw on his fingers while his damn hands were tied helpless.

But rats didn't hiss, and that had sounded a lot like a hiss.

It came again, and it was a hiss. The kind of shushing little hiss a person made warning someone to keep quiet.

Frowning, Collin lifted his head as best he could and craned his neck to look toward the noise. All he could see were shadows.

One of the shadows spoke to him. In a ghostly, thin whisper, it said, "You want loose of there, boy?"

The sound of it rasped icily along Collin's spine. He thought the voice of death would be like that, like a cold wind in dry leaves. But, flesh or spook, he didn't give a damn. Not if it meant to help him. He nodded vigorously.

The voice said, "Where's the money?"

"Loose me," Collin whispered. "I'll show you."

"You *tell* me. *Then* I'll loose you."

It was no time for arguing. Collin had to trust the shadow. He gave a jerk of his head toward a far corner. "Yonder."

"Yonder where?"

"Saddlebags piled up with the gear in that corner over there."

The shadow began to squirm toward the corner.

"Hey, let me loose!" Collin grunted.

Lyle made a noise and stirred in his sleep. Breath caught, Collin froze. Lyle began to snore again. The shadow whispered, "Shush, boy, you want to wake them?"

Collin swallowed hard. That was the next to last thing in the world he wanted. He lay back, waiting, hoping to hell the shadow was as good as its word. He hoped it was clever enough to do what it intended without waking anyone.

The stars stared down at him. The moon nudged an edge over the hole in the roof. As he watched, the visible bit of moon grew. The night seemed to be getting very old. And chilly.

Collin waited. There wasn't anything else he could do.

Something touched his hand. He flinched. The shadow, nearby him again, shushed him. He felt a

214

tugging at the cord that held the hand. He thought it was the steady tugging of a knife blade sawing against the cord. His heart seemed to jump at each tug.

The cord snapped.

The sudden release roused the pain in his back. Teeth clenched, hand fisted, he fought a groan, swallowing it down.

Fingers were prying open his fist. They put something into his hand, then pressed it closed again.

"Good luck, boy," the shadow whispered. And it slipped silently away.

It took Collin a couple of long deep breaths to collect himself. His arm had gone numb. Now it was turning all pins and needles. He lifted it awkwardly. Silhouetted against the sky, the object in his hand looked like an old-time Green River knife. Moonlight glinted along its honed blade.

Twisting his body and to hell with the pain, he got the blade onto the lashing that held his other wrist.

It wasn't easy to be cautiously quiet when he was in such a damn frantic hurry. He cut himself a couple of times. It didn't matter. He had to get loose, get away. Quick.

At last the hand was free.

He worked the numb fingers, then squirmed to get at the ropes on one ankle. Just as he slashed at it, he heard a noise from outside.

Bull coming in for a change of guard, he thought as he sprawled on his back. He shoved the knife under his body, then spread his arms as if he were still bound.

Bull strode in, gave him a glance, and went to wake Lyle. They grumbled together briefly while Lyle readied himself. Then Lyle took the carbine and went outside.

Bull rolled himself a smoke. He sat sucking on it, looking at Collin McKay. Finally he'd burned the quirly down to a butt. He pinched it out and stretched himself on his soogan up against the wall, and in a moment he was snoring.

Collin lay still, watching the moon haul its whole self into his range of vision. He counted Bull's snores. Counted a score of them before he ventured to sit up. He kept counting them as he cut at the rope on his ankle. Bull was still snoring steadily when the lashing finally gave. Collin turned the knife to the final bond. He was thinking ahead, wondering whether he should chance trying to steal a gun or concentrate on getting away as fast as he could, when suddenly all hell broke loose outside.

Lyle Bordeaux was still sluggish with sleep when he took his place at guard. He sat down on the ground, his back against the wall of the building, the carbine across his knees. Everything was quiet. He expected it would stay that way. He let his chin rest on his chest. His heavy eyelids closed. Pieces of dreams flitted through his mind.

A woman screamed.

Flinching, Lyle jerked to his feet. He flung the carbine up to his shoulder, aiming it toward the sound.

If it had been anything but the voice of a woman, he might have fired first and asked his questions later. But it was a woman, and as far as he knew, there was only one woman in these parts, besides Minnie. Minnie was inside, so the screamer must be that little whore, Weenie Greenwood. Lyle didn't figure there was any danger in her. Likely she was all upset by night spooks.

"Weenie!" he called at the darkness. "Weenie, is that you?"

Bull Bordeaux's dreams were troubled, filled with a sense of wrongness. The screams woke him from them with a start. His revolver was in his hand, his thumb automatically drawing back the hammer, as he scrambled up from his soogan.

It was a woman's scream. He thought instantly of Minnie Evans. But Minnie was there in the same room with him. He saw her sitting bolt upright, clutching her quilt to her breasts.

Lyle hollered something. Bull didn't hear it clearly. In his sleep-haze, he thought Lyle was in trouble. He heard Minnie gasp something at him as he dashed past her. He paid her no mind. Waving the gun, he lunged through the doorway.

The woman screamed again. And Lyle called again.

This time Bull heard the name that Lyle called. Of course, he thought, it would be that Greenwood woman. And Lyle wasn't in trouble at all. Bull grinned as his tension eased. But, as quickly as the grin formed, it faded. Something was wrong. As he'd run for the doorway, he'd seen something out of place. He'd heard Minnie gasp a warning of some kind. Wheeling, he looked back into the building. He saw Collin McKay.

* ★ ★

It was a woman's scream. It was Weenie, Collin thought. And for a long ugly moment, the thought froze him. Something had happened to Weenie. She needed help.

Bull Bordeaux came erupting from his soogan, waving his gun as he ran for the door. He didn't look toward Collin at all. And for an instant Collin thought he was gone, thought there was a chance. Eyes on the doorway, he slashed at the rope on his ankle.

Bull turned and looked through the doorway, directly at Collin.

It was too late to sprawl back, pretending to still be tied. Even if there'd been time, it wouldn't have worked. Minnie Evans was sitting up, staring at him.

There he was, in moonlight almost as bright as day, with the knife in his hand and one leg still bound to the fallen beam. He couldn't help Weenie. He couldn't help himself.

Bull leveled the gun at him. In the time it took a scear to release and a hammer to fall, lead would explode at him. It wouldn't miss. He'd be dead.

It'd be better than burning. Quick and clean. But, hell, he'd meant to escape. Goddammit, couldn't anything *ever* go right any more?

And Weenie. What would happen to Weenie? Dammit all!

Outside, the woman kept screaming for help. And Lyle kept hollering back for her to show herself.

CHAPTER
EIGHTEEN

Weenie offered to help. Stacy insisted on it. Reluctantly, Tuck allowed that he would need help. He discussed the plan with them, examining it and altering it until he felt it actually did have a chance of working.

The moon was well up, its light filtering through the forest canopy, when they moved. Leaving the horses tied, they headed toward the ruins of the trading post.

Together, they skirted the woods. Tuck found a place that suited him, a good spot for the women to hide. A large windfallen log would offer them solid cover. They could see over it into the L of the building.

He left them with strict instructions and with orders to run for the horses if anything went wrong. He had Stacy's promise that she'd obey. He hoped she would. No matter what, no matter why she had come with him, he wanted her to be safe and free.

He kissed her quickly before he left.

Cautiously, he crept back along the edge of the woods until he was opposite the window he'd looked into before. He knew there was a gun inside. And he knew there was an armed man.

The open expanse of land between the trees and the long wall of the ruins looked very broad, very bare, in the bright moonlight. Scanning it, Tuck wondered just what he was doing here like this. What was he really trying to prove? Who was he really trying to prove it to? It suddenly seemed like only a damned fool would worry about what another man thought of him, especially a man like Curly Hobbs. The thing that really mattered was what he thought of himself.

Dropping to his belly, he began to crawl across the field.

From their hiding place, Stacy and Weenie would be able to see him leave the woods. They'd be able to estimate when he reached the wall.

At the wall, he rose to his feet. He pressed himself flat, listening for a moment, before he chanced a glance inside.

Moonglow through the holes in the roof gave more light to the room than the small campfire had. He saw the rifle lying across a saddle on the floor. Someone was sleeping near it, rolled in a quilt. He thought that was the woman. Close under the window, he could hear snoring. That would be one of the Bordeaux men.

Weenie began to scream.

Instinctively, Tuck jerked back, away from the window. Breath held, he eased forward to look through it again.

He saw Bull Bordeaux on his feet, gun in hand, running toward the door. That was right, according to the plan. Bull dashed through the door.

Minnie Evans was sitting up, clutching her quilt to her breast. Tuck had hoped she'd jump and run at the sound of the scream, too. But she hadn't. He'd have to deal with her.

Hands on the sill, he vaulted through the window. His eyes were on the gun. He meant to have it. He had to have it. Landing on his feet, he lunged for it.

Minnie gasped at the sight of him.

Suddenly Bull Bordeaux was no longer outside. As Tuck launched himself through the window, Bull had turned. He was coming back into the room, the revolver in his hand cocked and leveled. But the gun wasn't aimed at Tuck. Not in that first instant. It pointed toward the far corner.

Tuck only glimpsed the figure of a man moonlit in the corner. Bull was turning. He'd seen Tuck. He was swinging the gun toward Tuck. His finger had already begun to tighten on the trigger. As he turned, the scear released.

Lead slammed into the wall at Tuck's side.

Tuck hit the ground, tumbled, came up onto his feet in a crouch. As he moved, his hand grabbed for the rifle. And missed.

Bull had the gun hammer back again. His finger was closing on the trigger again. This time he had the gun steady. It pointed at Tuck's chest.

In the moonlight, Tuck could see the black hole of the bore, darker than all the shadows. He could see the tension in Bull's hand.

He knew there was nowhere to go. No time to get there. Nothing existed in all the world but that black hole that would spit lead at him. Smash him all to hell and gone, and end everything.

He was thinking of Stacy. Wanting her. Hoping desperately that she'd run. Escape.

Bull grunted, a sudden sharp sound with pain in it. His hand jerked. The blast of gunpowder was a glare that burned its image into Tuck's eyes.

Minnie screamed.

Tuck realized with amazement that Bull had missed him. Even as he realized it, he was moving. Springing. Leaping past the gun to grapple with Bull. His arms locked around Bull's body, tense for the struggle.

But Bull wasn't struggling.

He was folding up. Going limp. Collapsing in Tuck's arms. The revolver slipped from his hand and thudded heavily on the ground.

Somebody let out a shout of elation.

For a startled moment, Tuck was holding Bull's weight against him. Staggering back, he let go. Bull crumpled at his feet.

The afterimage of the blast still hazed Tuck's vision. Through it, he saw the shape of a knife hilt rising from Bull's back. He saw the revolver Bull had dropped. As he bent to grab it, he glimpsed motion.

Suddenly the bulk of Lyle Bordeaux was filling the doorway. Lyle had a carbine in his hands. He swung its muzzle toward Tuck.

Snatching up Bull's revolver in his right hand, Tuck slammed the heel of his left at the hammer. The gun bucked in his grip.

Lyle flinched as the carbine jerked hard in his hands. Steadying it, he squeezed the trigger.

There was no blast of sound, no glare of flame.

With a curse, Lyle tugged at the lever. It wouldn't move.

Tuck's hand was already slapping again at the gun hammer. And again. The blaze of gunshots blurred together.

Lyle tottered. Dark smears appeared on his shirt. Still, he stood. Cursing, he jerked at the lever again. The carbine was jammed. Tuck's first shot had nicked the action. Grasping the gun by the barrel, Lyle swung it like a club.

Tuck's hand was striking the hammer again. He felt it fall. He heard a dull click as it hit an empty casing. He saw the butt of the carbine smashing toward his face. He tried to duck.

The explosion of light inside his skull overrode the afterimage of gunfire. It overwhelmed everything. It swallowed him, sucking him down into darkness.

Collin McKay huddled behind the fallen beam, the sounds of too many gunshots pounding around him. Then the shooting stopped and there was only the smell of burned powder and the fear.

Nothing more happened.

Slowly he became aware of the awkwardness of his position and the dull pain in his shoulder. Warily, he lifted his head enough to look over the beam.

There were four limp mounds, four bodies, among the shadows. Shifting enough to ease the ache, Collin gazed at them.

Bull Bordeaux lay face down, with the hilt of the Green River knife sticking out of his back. That was a hell of a fine throwing knife, Collin thought, remembering the feel of it in his hand, the easy balance of it as he'd sent it flying.

In the moonlight blood looked black. The smear on the front of Minnie Evans's chemise was dark and ugly. As he'd ducked for cover, Collin had seen her jerked back by the bullet, and heard her scream. It was Bull's shot, the one meant for the sheriff.

That poor damn fool of a sheriff, Collin thought. He should have stayed with his woman instead of pressing on so damn determined. He should never have tried to take on both the Bordeaux brothers. Collin reckoned he'd had his reasons. Maybe they'd been worth dying for. Collin hoped so. He felt sorry about the sheriff. Despite it all, he'd kind of liked Tuck Tobin.

He looked at the bodies, grateful that he wasn't lying limp now himself. He'd come close. Awful damn close. But he was still alive, and the bullet wound in his shoulder didn't seem serious, and with luck he might manage to stay alive for years and years to come.

Luck was a damn strange thing. He never wanted to press his so close again. From now on, he meant to stay clear of trouble, never take such damn chances again. Live quiet and peaceful and die real old in a feather bed.

He thought suddenly of Weenie. The screams he'd heard had sounded like her voice. They'd stopped. What had happened to her? He had to get loose and find her.

He fingered the cord that still held his leg to the beam. His hands were shaking. He tugged at a knot. It was tighter than a banker's purse strings. He needed a way to cut it. A knife.

There was a knife. It was in Bull Bordeaux's back.

Collin squirmed over the beam and stretched out on his belly. He stretched as far as he could, pulling at the bound ankle. The knife was beyond his reach. But Bull Bordeaux's outflung arm wasn't. Collin managed to lock a hand around Bull's wrist. He tried to budge the body. It was like trying to drag a dead horse. And it made his shoulder hurt. Teeth clenched, he tried again.

Bull groaned.

Startled, Collin gulped a breath that stuck in his throat. He felt tendons move in the wrist he was grasping. As he jerked his trembling hand away, he saw Bull's fingers flex.

Bull's face was toward him. Moonlight shone on the eyes as they opened. They gazed unfocused, then sharpened on Collin.

"McKay," Bull grunted. "Goddamn you."

Huffing, Bull got his arms under him. He lifted his body and got himself onto his hands and knees. He swung his head from side to side like an injured animal, pained and bewildered and angry. Ready to charge anything that moved, come hell or lead.

"McKay," he said. "I'll kill you."

Collin swallowed at the lump in his throat. Finding his voice took effort. "No, Bull. You're dead. You're dead and gone to hell, and I'm the devil come to torment you."

"Hell," Bull muttered, swinging his big head. He stopped suddenly and squinted at the banked embers

225

of the campfire. As he dragged himself toward it, he grumbled, "Kill you, McKay."

Collin jerked at his bound leg. He felt the fallen beam rock slight. But it wouldn't move. He damn sure couldn't haul himself away and it with him. He had to get loose.

The knife was still in Bull's back, taunting Collin as Bull worked his way to the embers.

Bull brushed at the banked fire with his bare hand. If it burned him, he didn't seem to notice. Lowering his head, he blew on the coals. They answered with little tongues of flame.

Bull sat back on his heels. He pulled a burning stick out of the fire and threw it toward Collin.

The stick turned end over end, losing its flame. Its head was a vivid coal as it flew past Collin. It fell in the jumble of splintered shingles behind him. Twisting, he tried to grab it, but it was out of reach. And as he struggled to get it, the splinters were taking fire.

There was plenty of tinder. The whole building was full of it. Rubble from the fallen roof. Dead dry weeds that had blown in. The walls themselves. Dead dry walls.

Bull was throwing more sticks. Then he was scooping glowing embers with his bare hands, scattering them wildly around him. To every side, flames were taking hold. Growing.

"You're crazy!" Collin shouted at him.

"Hell!" Bull said. And he laughed.

The laugh stopped suddenly. Bull gurgled as if it had snagged deep in his chest. Slowly, he fell forward onto

226

the fire. The little tongues of flame began to work at his shirt.

For one long drawn breath, Collin stared at him. Then there was a smell of scorching meat. And Collin knew he damn well had to get loose and get out of there, or Bull would have had his way after all.

Fire burned. Not just flesh, but ropes as well. Wrenching around, Collin spotted a piece of burning wood that was within his reach. He snatched it and thrust the flaming end at the cord that held him to the fallen beam.

The room was filling with smoke. It stung his eyes and rasped his throat. He blinked and coughed as he bent over the rope. He was intent on the flame that was slowly burning through it when he heard the voice. It scared hell out of him, speaking his name.

"McKay?" Tuck Tobin said incredulously. "But you're dead."

Collin squinted at the figure staggering through the smoke toward him. There was blood on Tobin's face. In the fireglow, his eyes were glassy. Unreal.

It was Doomsday, Collin thought, and all the dead were walking and this was hell burning and he himself was dead even if he didn't know it.

But that was damn foolishness. Tobin had been unconscious, not dead. Now he was awake. They were both alive.

As much to himself as to Tobin, he said, "I'm not dead. But I got to get loose. I got to get out of here quick or I will be."

Dazed, Tobin said vaguely, "Weenie told me you were dead."

"Weenie!" Collin looked up at him. "Is she all right?"

"Uh huh. I left her with Stacy. Both all right."

Collin started to say something else. He stopped short as the cord snapped. Free, he scrambled to his feet. But suddenly he was giddy and the pain was clawing at his shoulder again. For a moment he thought he was going to fall. But the giddiness passed. Catching his breath, he started for the door.

"McKay," Tobin called at him. "The others . . . the Bordeaux brothers . . . the woman . . ."

"Bull's dead for sure," Collin answered. The body of Lyle Bordeaux lay at the doorway. Pausing, Collin touched Lyle's face. He added, "So's Lyle."

Tuck had found Minnie Evans. He said, "The woman's still alive. Help me with her."

Collin wanted out. He felt weak and shaky, hardly able to take care of himself. He was scared. He didn't give a damn about Minnie Evans. Or the fool sheriff either, he told himself as he looked back at Tuck Tobin.

Tuck was trying to drag Minnie to the door. He was having trouble. And the flames were spreading fast. In minutes the whole building would be blazing.

Muttering a curse at himself, Collin turned back. Tuck had a grip under Minnie's arms. Collin caught her ankles. Lifting her hurt his back. He wondered why the hell he was doing it. She groaned as they carried her toward the doorway.

★   ★   ★

228

At the edge of the woods, Stacy and Weenie huddled together. Weenie's screams had succeeded in drawing the Bordeaux brothers' attention — for a moment. But one brother had run back into the building. There'd been shooting. The other brother ran in, and there was more shooting.

Weenie no longer screamed. The night was silent now, the moonlight white and cold against the blackness of the shadows. In the angle of the building, the picketed horses stirred restlessly.

Watching, Stacy waited.

Tuck had ordered her to stay away from the building, no matter what happened. He'd said if it all went well, he'd call her when it was done. If it went wrong, she was to get the hell away. Run. Forget it all.

She knew she could never do that. Even if she ran and managed to escape, she could never forget. For the first time, she knew without a doubt what really mattered to her. Not the money. Not her notions of freedom. Not anything in the world except Tuck Tobin.

She waited.

Nothing was happening. There was no sign of Tuck. No sign of the Bordeaux brothers.

Nothing.

She couldn't stand it any longer. She had to know.

"You stay here and keep still," she told Weenie. "I've got to see what's happened."

"But Tuck said —"

"Weenie, he may need me. You wait. Or go back to the horses. Understand?"

Weenie nodded. "I understand. If it were Collin —"

She snuffled, and Stacy touched her shoulder. Then, stealthily, Stacy began to work her way across the weeded open toward the old building.

Something glimmered within the building. An orange glow flickered through a window. It was growing. Spreading. A fireglow. The smell of smoke tainted the air.

A horse reared, pawing frantically. Another horse jerked back, tugging against the picket line. The line snapped. Snorting, a horse bolted. The others followed.

Flames reached through the windows.

Stacy ran toward the building, shouting Tuck's name. Screaming for him.

Frightened, Weenie came chasing after her.

As Stacy neared the doorway, she saw Tuck. Then another man. They staggered out of the burning building, carrying something between them. She raced to them as they dragged their burden clear of the building and lowered it to the ground. As Tuck turned toward her, she flung herself into his arms.

There was blood on his face. She touched his cheek. Her fingertips traced the bloodstain to the gash on his forehead. "You're hurt!"

"No, I'm fine," he said, grinning. His arms wrapped around her.

Collin stood with his legs splayed, exhausted, alive. Weenie stared at him. She gasped a small thin breath and threw herself at him.

As she came against him, he stumbled back and lost his balance. He fell, and she fell with him, her arms

230

around his neck. She was laughing and crying as she clung to him.

Lying on the ground, unnoticed, Minnie Evans stirred. Her eyes opened. She squinted at the flaming building. Slowly her expression of puzzlement turned to horror.

Lurching to her feet, she lunged toward the doorway.

Collin saw her. He shouted, "Minnie, stop!"

She ran.

Tuck pulled away from Stacy. He leaped to grab for Minnie. But she'd reached the doorway and was plunging inside. As he started after her, something blasted like a cannonshot. With a rumbling crash, roof beams and blazing shingles came smashing down, blocking his way.

"Good God!" he muttered, staring at the flaming wreckage.

The fierce heat surged over him, forcing him back. He returned to Stacy's side.

Catching his hand in hers, she asked him, "Why?"

He shook his head.

"The money," Collin said.

"It was in there?"

He nodded. The money *had* been in there. A shadow had stolen it. A shadow that had saved Collin's life, and the sheriff's as well. It was the shadow's knife that had stopped Bull Bordeaux from slamming lead into Tobin. Collin figured he and Tobin both owed the shadow for that. Let the law think the money had burned.

"I don't reckon there's much in there now besides ashes," he said. He wondered what the old galoot would do with all that money. A man really couldn't ask much more of life than to live that long and grow that sly and ornery and get a fistful of cash like that to boot. Unless it was a good woman. Maybe a good woman was better than a fistful of money. He gave Weenie a squeeze.

Sadly, she murmured, "Thirty thousand dollars, all gone."

"Forget it, sugar," he told her. "Money ain't worth dying for."

She glanced at the flames and shuddered. Faintly, she said, "Minnie must have been crazy."

"They were all crazy," Collin said. "Now they're all dead."

"We're alive." Weenie looked into his face. Her mouth reached for his.

Tuck and Stacy stood together, hand in hand, watching wordlessly as the fire reached its peak, then began to wane.

After a while, Tuck looked at Stacy. She met his eyes. Her lips parted slightly in invitation.

But there was still a question hanging between them. Tuck asked, "What now?"

"What do you mean?"

"The money's gone. It's gone forever now. And I don't have anything to offer you. I'm going to quit my job. I won't run for sheriff again. I'm going away, somewhere else, to something different. I don't know what. I'm forty years old, and I'm starting over from nothing. Stacy, will you go with me?"

"Yes."

He caught her into his arms. Held her. Kissed her. A long deep kiss.

Collin nudged Weenie. He gestured toward Tuck and Stacy. Weenie looked at the two of them, then at Collin. He gave a jerk of his head toward the forest. She nodded.

Cautiously, quietly, he got himself to his feet. Holding Weenie's hand, he led her toward the woods.

Ducking into the secret darkness of the trees, Collin sighed with relief. Maybe they'd make it after all.

"Weenie," he whispered, "you think you'd like to be a poor dirt farmer's wife?"

"I don't think I'd be very good at it," she said sadly.

"Likely I wouldn't be a very good farmer, either," he allowed. Reluctantly, he suggested, "How about a bank robber's wife?"

"It's not the money," she told him. "I just don't think I want to be married."

"Not to me?"

"Not to anybody. But I'd like to have a regular man of my own."

He squeezed her hand. "How'd you like to go to Canada?"

"I'd love it."

Suddenly, from behind, they heard Tuck Tobin shout, "McKay, goddammit, this time don't steal *all* the horses!"

Riding double on the bay, Stacy and Tuck headed for Morrison. From there he could telegraph his story, and his resignation, to Jack Hollow. And then on to somewhere else. They agreed they'd decide where when they got there.

As he loped his cayuse toward Jack Hollow, Pike was thinking of Ida Red and pink silk sheets. He was aching weary, longing for rest.

Getting old, he allowed to himself. Maybe it was time he gave up the roving life and settled with a roof over his head. Ida Red had one hell of a fine roof.

Only a man just wouldn't feel right if he didn't put meat in the pot now and then himself. He thought he might get a job in town. Doing what, he wondered. Sure as hell not swamping out stores or the like.

There was almost thirty thousand dollars in the saddlebags he carried. Ida didn't need that money. She already had more than she could ever spend. It was just the fun of getting what everybody else was after that had excited her. Once she had the money, Pike thought, she might be agreeable to turning it back to the bank.

He'd proved himself once by bringing in the robber, McKay. If he did it again now by bringing back the money, he reckoned, the townsfolk would look right favorable on him. Might be he'd declare in the coming election and run for sheriff.

Why not?

He was damned sure a man of his horse sense and experience could easily beat out a mule colt like that young Curly Hobbs.

Chuckling at the notion, he rode on.

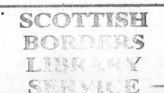